FICTION OF
THE FIRST WORLD WAR

FICTION OF THE FIRST WORLD WAR
A Study

George Parfitt

faber and faber

LONDON · BOSTON

First published in 1988
by Faber and Faber Limited
3 Queen Square London WC1N 3AU

Filmset by Wilmaset Birkenhead Wirral

Printed in Great Britain by
Richard Clay Ltd Bungay Suffolk

British Library Cataloguing in Publication Data

Parfitt, George
Fiction of the First World War: *a study*.
1. English fiction – 20th century – History and criticism.
2. World War, 1914–1918 – Literature and the War
I. Title
823′.912′09358   PR830.W65
ISBN 0-571-14896-4

In an age when critical theory promises, or threatens, to 'cross over' into literature and to become its own object of study, there is a powerful case for reasserting the primacy of the literary text. These studies are intended in the first instance to provide substantial critical introductions to writers of major importance. Although each contributor inevitably writes from a considered critical position, it is not the aim of the series to impose a uniformity of theoretical approach. Each book will make use of biographical material and each will conclude with a select bibliography which will in all cases take note of the latest developments usefully relevant to the subject. Beyond that, however, contributors have been chosen for their critical abilities as well as for their familiarity with the subject of their choice.

Although the primary aim of the series is to focus attention on individual writers, there will be exceptions. And although the majority of writers or periods studied will be of the twentieth century, this is not intended to preclude other writers or periods. Above all, the series aims to return readers to a sharpened awareness of those texts without which there would be no criticism.

John Lucas

In memory of my uncles
Franklin George Ekins (d. 1918)
Willingham Richard Ekins (d. 1917)
Thomas Arbuthnot Ekins (d. 1926)
who fought in the First World War.

Contents

Preface

I should like to thank the General Editor of this series, John Lucas, for asking me to write this book, for his comments on my draft and for many conversations over the years. I should like to thank my wife, Maureen Bell, for many things. Above all, perhaps, on this occasion I should like to thank the students at the University of Nottingham who taught me in seminars I held on the literature of the First World War over several years.

Editions used are identified in the text on their first appearance. Full details are given in the bibliography at the end of the book.

Much of the material on Frederic Manning first appeared in *The Journal of Commonwealth Literature* XVI no. 1: I am grateful to its editors for permission to reuse this material.

Introduction

The First World War was the first major European war after the conflict between Prussia and France in 1870. Britain was drawn into a continental war for the first time since the Crimea (1853–6) and the war was to prove very unlike the rather humiliating conflict with the Boers in 1899–1902. Some people, considering the evidence of the Fashoda incident (1898) and of the German Naval Law (1900), had felt that a major European war was inevitable, but many argued that, on the contrary, such a war was impossible among civilized nations, this latter view being most famously advanced by Norman Angell in his book *The Great Illusion* of 1910. And while it may be natural for British writers to emphasize the role of Britain and her empire in the Great War it is important to remember that France, Belgium, Russia and Germany all suffered more than Britain did. Even when remembering the hardships of the German naval blockade, and without belittling the psychological sufferings of the home front, it should be recalled that British land was not devastated as happened in other European countries.

This is not the place for a detailed account of the causes of the war.[1] Its formal cause is well known – the assassination of the Archduke Ferdinand of Austria at Sarajevo. Austria's ultimatum to Serbia led to other nations lining up in accordance with existing treaties, and Britain (having kept her participation in doubt until quite late) was drawn in by the German violation of Belgium's neutrality. But such formal causes say little in themselves and we need to look further to gain some understanding of why the various nations were prepared to fight in 1914. There can, for instance, be little doubt that Germany was eager to gain more 'room in the sun'. Britain, still perhaps the most powerful country on earth, with its extraordinary empire, was both envied by Germany and suspicious of German ambitions. France was eager for a chance to avenge the humiliations of 1870 and Russia to compensate for the setback of her recent war with Japan. An armaments build-up contributed to tension and the way in which these and other strands combined to produce a war which was a watershed in western civilization is well indicated by noticing that the First World War was both the last major dynastic war in Europe and a war for markets which was also the showpiece of new technology.

This was a mass war, both in terms of the numbers who took part and of casualties. Some nations were represented by brigades of volunteers, but the main participating countries were involved to an unprecedented degree, not so much because of conscription, which was not new (except in Britain) as because of the length and scale of the war. It is possible to try to reduce the impact of the carnage by speaking, say, of the rate of loss of single regiments at Waterloo, but this is beside the point. The rate of loss in the First World War (which should be enough for anyone) has to be understood in relation to how that rate was sustained over a long period. It is, in fact, hard to think of any time since the Black Death in the fourteenth century when Europe had suffered so much. The war, therefore, could hardly fail to be a test on many levels. It tested German ambition and organization, the strength of the French desire for revenge on Germany, the residual power of Tsarist Russia, the strength of Britain and her empire, and the nature of the United States' commitment to an international role. The war also tested established ways of fighting and new ways of killing. It tested the morale of volunteers and conscripts, the endurance and versatility of women. It went on for a long time and over vast tracts of land.

The tissue of alliances which had been seen as a way of preventing wars became a pattern of commitments to conflict, and one of the ways in which the war may be associated with ideas of failure is that in which forces opposed to war did little to prevent it. Worker internationalism, which some had thought would make war a fiasco, with workers refusing to fill their role of gunfodder, collapsed at once, while large sections of the international movement for women's suffrage went the same way into the patriotism that kills. Atavistic greeds and prejudices proved much superior to ideals of international co-operation.

The war was a failure on other levels also. The humiliations imposed on Germany at the Treaty of Versailles probably did much to prepare the ground for Nazism and the Second World War, while that new attempt at internationalism represented by the League of Nations was seen as a failure well before 1945. The war hastened the coming of revolution in Russia and breached isolationism in the United States, yet in neither case can the change be seen as an unqualified success. Then there is the matter of individual expectations which were not fulfilled. The war increased contact between people of different classes, especially at the front, and it provided new opportunities for women. But, recalling slogans about a land fit for heroes (and heroines) or about a war to end war, it is hard to avoid feeling that the war was a success for very few, and those mainly non-combatants. It is the bodies and the bereaved who dominate, the physically devastated, the mental cases and the alcoholics. In the preface to R. H. Mottram's *Ten Years Ago* (1928) W. E. Bates writes about the silence, in post-war years, of men who had fought, saying:

> It has been a significant silence, like those two brief minutes on Armistice Day, and just as definitely it has meant 'never again'.

Sadly, this war, allegedly fought to make war impossible, did no such thing. It settled little and left Germany with revenge on its agenda. Because there was some kind of survival it encouraged people to feel that even on such a scale war was acceptable, while the pressures of the war encouraged the technology of mass slaughter, and there are always those who itch to test new weapons, preferably in battle conditions . . .

This short book is about how some novelists treated aspects of the war. It is both helped and handicapped by the sparseness of secondary writing on the subject, for while much has been written about the verse which came from the war its fiction has been neglected. This neglect has come about partly because of the difficulty of defining the limits of the subject. There is no adequate bibliography of fiction of the war and this hints at the problems of defining which novels should be included and which excluded, some of these problems being more formidable than others. At what point does a novel which takes account of the war become a novel *of* the war? When does a novel become a memoir? Should novels which concentrate primarily upon aspects of the war's effect at home be included, or novels concerned with how the war shaped post-war life? If the field is restricted to novels in English, should one exclude novels in English by Americans, Australians and Indians (among others)? Should the material be approached on its own terms or in relation to views about the history of the novel form?

This book is too brief to allow for much consideration of the niceties of such questions; and the decisions I have made have been practical rather than theoretical. My concern is, in part, to suggest here that much more work needs to be done before an adequate view of the novel's treatment of, and response to, the war can be reached. I shall restrict myself to novels written in English by writers who are themselves British (with one exception, the Australian Frederic Manning), although I make passing reference to German and French fiction. Some of the novels were written by combatants, others by non-combatants; some were written by authors who had written fiction before the war and others by authors made novelists by the war. All the novels I discuss, with again one exception, Rebecca West, are by men, for reasons touched on in my conclusion.

The scale of the war made any idea of a novel which could be an adequate overview absurd. Tolstoy had come to feel that Napoleon's Russian campaign was too vast for such an overview, and the Great War was a much larger conflict than that. The novels which can be seen as products of that war vary greatly in range and ambition, but a general feature worth noting is that there is a marked tendency to fragmentation, to books frankly offered as records of moments and aspects of war experience. Another way of putting this would be to say that the novelists who try to say something about the war are led to adopt a variety of angles of vision and types of fictional approach. This variety can only affect what they 'say' about the war, and it also affects their ways of articulating their visions. Some novelists, as we shall see, seem anxious to pretend that old styles and old forms are still adequate for writing about the war, while others are clear that the occasion calls for innovation.

On this matter of how novelists approached the task of writing about the war it is worth emphasizing that English fiction in the two decades which preceded the war was rich and various. At the 'serious' level fiction during these decades is dominated by Gissing, Hardy, Conrad, Wells, Forster, Bennett and James. Lawrence had most of his major work to come in 1914 and Joyce's volume of short stories, *Dubliners,* was published in the year the war began. Kipling, a short-story writer and poet rather than a novelist, should be mentioned because of the impact of his writing upon novelists of the war. The only point I want to make here is that the dominant novelists of the period before the war offer a variety of approaches to the writing of fiction and that they cannot reasonably be seen as voices of an establishment. Kipling can be seen as an analyst of establishment voices. Bennett and Gissing make use of provincial or outsider voices, while Hardy (who stopped writing novels after *Jude the Obscure* in 1895) is country- rather than city-centred and Conrad is a Pole, James an American. Several of these writers are clearly patriotic, and the nostalgic elements in Forster's *Howard's End* (1910) were, as we shall see, echoed in the English fiction of the war, but the most significant tradition of the novel immediately before the war is one of analysis and independence.

Men and women who write about the Great War are seeking, for whatever reasons, to present some kind of truth about a conflict which was fought in several theatres, across thousands of miles, over several years and with vast armies. But it was also a war of which most combatants saw very little and over which they had almost no control. On the one hand the war seems to call for epic treatment, but, on the other, it defeats this possibility and drives writers towards the modest scale of letters, lyrics and memoirs. There is a point at which fiction merges with memoir (see Extended Notes, p. 142), and a case can be made for regarding works like the memoirs of Blunden, Sassoon and Graves as fiction. On the other hand there are a number of novels of the war which use the memoir's convention of offering a life as an account of literal truth. Most English novels of the war implicitly admit their fragmented viewpoints by representing the outlook of a single soldier (most usually an officer of medium rank) or, at most, of a group of front-line men. Similarly, novels which concentrate on the home front represent domestic reactions. But one well-known English novel of the war could be said to attempt something like an overview, since its protagonist is a general.

C. S. Forester was an experienced professional novelist by the time *The General* was published in 1936, his first novel, *Payment Deferred,* having come out ten years before. Not only is the book unusual in having a staff officer as its focus but it is also a distinctly difficult novel to pin down, at least once its structural and narrative confidence has been acknowledged.

The General is basically an orthodox sequential story, but it does not begin with its protagonist's birth or end with his death – or at least not literally. Instead Forester uses a framing device, so that the book begins and ends in the same present: 'Nowadays Lieutenant-General Sir Herbert Curzon, KCMG, CB, DSO, is just one of Bournemouth's seven generals . . .'; and 'now Lieutenant-General Sir Herbert Curzon and his wife, Lady Emily, are frequently to be seen on the promenade at Bournemouth . . .' (Penguin, 1979, pp. 5, 234). After the two opening paragraphs, however, which establish Curzon at Bournemouth, Forester goes back to 'The day on which Curzon first stepped over the threshold of history . . .' and his novel then works forward towards the Bournemouth conclusion. Since the story is of the rise of Curzon in the army and consequently in society, he might be said to have been born when he 'stepped over the threshold of history' and to have died when he received the wound which put him out of the army, for the army is his life. Few novels of the war are concerned with professional soldiers and since Forester has a protagonist who is a career soldier of total dedication it is appropriate that the structure is defined by the career, although the author does filter in information which makes it clear that the general has humble origins. As Curzon rises in the army he has the opportunity to marry above his social class and becomes an intimate of those who have political and social power, rejecting his origins and accepting the decorations which the establishment gives. But Curzon, unlike Ford Madox Ford's General Campion in his Tietjens novels, has no political ambitions of his own. He is a military man who is loyal to his political bosses, and until his wound he is a lucky man, his rise coming about through chance rather than

[8]

virtue. Curzon's perspective is that of the faithful officer who carries out the orders of his superiors by giving orders to his inferiors and seeing that these are obeyed.

Since Curzon is a man who rises from obscurity to prominence and who earns honourable retirement he might be seen as a quasi-official voice of the nation at war, but there are difficulties here. Curzon's perspective, first of all, is that of the General Staff and he knows little about rankers or even of subalterns, the latter being the most usual protagonists of English novels of the front. Curzon can only 'speak for' the nation as defined by the powers controlling the war effort, and he shows qualities which make him the proper tool of such powers, for Curzon is not very intelligent, clinging to a few inflexible certitudes. He could easily become a caricature, an obvious target for Sassoon's satirical poems of the war; and the real difficulty of *The General* comes when one tries to assess how Curzon should be viewed. The framing device suggests pathos rather than apotheosis and the novel's tone is often ambiguous. A reader is often asked to observe Curzon rather than to engage with him. So we are told at the end of chapter 20 that 'Curzon did his duty with all his nerve and strength, as was his way, while the higher command looked on him with growing approval; he was a man after their own heart, who allowed no consideration to impede him in the execution of his orders' (p. 196). This seems to allow the reader either to look at Curzon with higher command eyes or to take an independent and critical view. It is not easy to forget that Curzon's kind of duty reduced flexible thinking in the war and that the Haig principle cost many lives which might have been saved. Moreover, total obedience was to be the Nuremberg

[9]

defence. Phrases like 'stepped over the threshold of history' can be read as serious, if slightly portentous, or as mildly ironic; and what is to be made of a man 'adjusting his mind to the business of commanding a brigade' who was 'ready for the responsibility in ten seconds' (p. 48)? Should we be awed and heartened, or horrified? The cover of the text I am using has a reproduction of a portrait in that military style which seems to get surfaces exactly right and yet to suggest absolutely nothing about anything beneath the skin, but the back of my text quotes the *Observer*'s reviewer as saying 'I think that this is the most penetrating and subtle study of a Regular Army officer that I have ever read.' Perhaps, however, the two are not incompatible. Forester's cool, detached authorial voice admits of an ironical reading of the novel, and the final lines suggest something close to futility in the 'old-maidish smile', the bad game of bridge and the 'irascibility when the east wind blows' (p. 234). The point may be that there seems to be little beyond the surface because there *is* little, and that this emptying of the personality is what the professional army needs.

But if the army calls for this, the question which comes to mind is who asks the army to be like this, and the answer must be 'society'. In so far as this is true the Curzons are needed and are heroic, just as the drained but obedient private is a necessity of a society at war. By this account even the marked element of cliché in *The General* is functional: Curzon is a cliché, but a necessary one, given the postulates which make for war. The enigmatic nature of *The General* is well caught by the entry for Forester in *Twentieth Century Authors* which says that the novel is 'a dispassionate study of the mentality and behavior of some of the higher command', but goes on to claim that Forester

[10]

himself was puzzled by the book's popularity in Germany until he learnt that 'it was regarded by the Nazis as a sublime deification of the militaristic spirit' (ed. S. Kunitz and H. Haycroft, Wilson, 1942).

Perhaps there is some connection, then, between the enigmatic quality of *The General* and the rank of its protagonist. It might also be suggested that Curzon empties his personality to keep a sense of purpose and integrity. The war makes sense to him because of his rigid concept of duty. Finding a pattern was never easy, however, for volunteers with less power than Curzon had.

I

Some Patterns

The Great War has, at least so far as the Western Front is concerned, a dominant shape – that of the trench – and yet it was in some ways a shapeless war, its lasting images those of almost indistinguishable mud and corpses, of landscapes deprived of form, and of vast numbers of combatants. But all writing is an attempt at significant form, and novelists who wrote of this war had to seek patterns which might help to make sense of the phenomenon. The most common basic pattern used is that of the life of a single protagonist: this chapter looks at three other patterns, all inherited from pre-war, which were used to give value to this basic shape.

1. The Great War as pilgrimage

The idea that human life is a voyage is perhaps as old as literature, and from the beginning this includes, as in the *Odyssey,* the suggestion that to make a voyage is to be physically and morally tested. When the image of life-as-voyage is given an explicitly religious dimension we have the idea of pilgrimage and the testing becomes more and more psychological. As late as Bunyan's *Pilgrim's Progress* and Fielding's *Tom Jones* the sense of the external test remains strong, but by Bunyan's time the pressure of Calvinism means that the moral and spiritual dimensions of the voyage are recognizably what we would call psychological. Christian's testing is as much an image of humankind struggling with inner temptation as with outer, and we are well on the way to the nineteenth century's concern with the pilgrimage as an account of inner struggle.

It is hardly surprising that writings about the Great War make use of the image of life as a journey. Soldiers travelled to the war from their homes and, although the war was dominated by that seemingly fixed feature, the trench, the experience of serving in the line nevertheless involved journeys between the front, reserve and rest lines; between one part of the front and another; from trench over parapet in attack. Also, of course, going to the war meant responding to tests and challenges – the call of King and Country, the appeal of 'little Belgium', the more intimate challenges of women, the fear of shame and the call of comradeship.

The key text here is *Pilgrim's Progress,* one of those writings known in some form by many with little literary interest or experience. Bunyan's book treats of hope as well as the weakness of human beings, and a soldier who knew the story might often think of himself as being in the Slough of Despond. Yet he would also know that, if he continued to face his task, he might reach the Heavenly City, even if this hope proved to be no more than the interlude of rest at the beginning of Remarque's *All Quiet on the Western Front.*

Two brief examples will suggest how deeply embedded *Pilgrim's Progress* is in the literature of the war. The first comes in W. F. Morris's novel *Bretherton:*

Approaching the mess in the dark was a hazardous undertaking, for one had to steer through a small

[13]

archway between two barns and cross a farm courtyard
by a narrow path bordered by a very large and juicy
midden. One false step and one was in the slough of
despond. (Odhams, n.d., p. 315)

An interesting verbal sequence seems to have sprung
the allusion: 'Approaching . . . hazardous undertaking
. . . steer . . . narrow path . . . midden . . . false step . . .'
But when the allusion arrives it is low key (with no
capitalization) and perfunctory. Clearly the reference
to the Slough of Despond here is an isolated moment
rather than part of a reading of the war in Bunyan's
terms. Something similar occurs in 'Ian Hay's' very
popular *The First Hundred Thousand,* an early fictional account of a journey to the front. In chapter 18 a
private acting as guide leads 'a dolorous procession'
which embarks on a 'laboured progress'. After a
confused halt, 'With resigned grunts the weary pil-
grims hoisted themselves and their numerous burdens
out of their slimy thoroughfare . . . and proceeded upon
their dolorous way' (Blackwood, 1916, pp. 242–3). Here
again the references seem subconscious, almost casual.
It is interesting that the awareness of Bunyan surfaces
at a time of crisis, but the allusions fade out and the
novel does not, overall, imagine its journey in Bunyan's
terms. There are, however, two major fictions of the
war which do: John Buchan's *Mr Standfast* and Henry
Williamson's *The Patriot's Progress.*
  Buchan's title, of course, immediately suggests a
connection with Bunyan, but a reader of *Mr Standfast*
is soon made aware that *Pilgrim's Progress* is to be of
more than passing significance. Thus, in the opening
chapter, we are told of Peter Pienaar, a pro-British
Boer, air ace now German captive, 'a cripple after five
months of blazing glory'. In captivity Pienaar 'had

[14]

discovered the pleasures of reading' and 'Somehow or other . . . had got a *Pilgrim's Progress,* from which he seemed to extract enormous pleasure' ((1919), Pan, 1964, p. 15). Buchan later underlines the fact that Bunyan's book is to be seen as a consolation to Pienaar in his captivity: it, with the Bible, helped with his reflections (p. 141). Further, Buchan indicates that *Pilgrim's Progress* is to be central to his plot, when, early in the novel, Mary tells Richard Hannay 'Buy tomorrow a copy of the *Pilgrim's Progress* and get it by heart. You will receive letters and messages some day and the style of our friends is apt to be reminiscent of John Bunyan' (p. 23).[1] Thereafter Bunyan reappears regularly: as Blenkiron tells Hannay 'This is a rough business and we won't bring in the name of a gently reared and pure-minded young girl. If we speak of her at all we call her by a pet name out of the *Pilgrim's Progress*'; as the Scot Amos claims to be a 'great reader of the *Pilgrim's Progress*'; as Bunyan's text is used for a clue, and so on (pp. 44, 64, 71).

It is obvious, however, that Buchan wants his readers to feel that the use of Bunyan informs more than just the plot of *Mr Standfast.* The title encourages us to see the adventure as analogous to Bunyan's fiction, and there is no doubt that this is an analogy we are meant to accept as a valid reading of the war. When, for example, Hannay is unravelling the plot on 'The Skirts of the Coolin' (chapter 6) he is operating in difficult territory: 'I found myself slithering among screes, climbing steep chimneys, and travelling precariously along razor-backs.' Since he has got the *Pilgrim's Progress* by heart it is not perhaps surprising that, when he has reached his 'cache' and has begun to retrace his steps, he thinks 'that I must be very like the picture of Christian on the title-page of my *Pilgrim's*

[15]

Progress. I was liker Christian before I reached my destination – Christian after he had got up the Hill Difficulty' (pp. 93–4). And although this passage is partly wry humour, it is quickly evident that the comparison is seriously meant. When Mary meets Hannay at Bullivant's house we have the following:

> 'Good evening, General Hannay. You got over the Hill Difficulty.'
> 'The next stage is the Valley of Humiliation,' I answered . . . (p. 144)

After this the connections are made again and again, with the emphasis falling particularly on Mary as Faithful and Richard as Christian. Mary herself makes the latter identification explicit:

> 'You look a tremendous warrior, Dick. I have never seen you like this before. I was in Doubting Castle and very much afraid of Giant Despair, till you came.' (p. 172)

It is Peter Pienaar, however, who seeks to be Standfast (p. 209) and Pienaar who is the focus for the final Bunyan allusions.

When Pienaar is taken from the wreckage of the plane in which he offers his final sacrifice, 'In his pocket was his old battered *Pilgrim's Progress*'[2] and the next morning Hannay reads from Bunyan's book, choosing from it words as 'a salute and farewell' to this 'soldier of Britain'. But Pienaar is now seen not as Mr Standfast, 'whom he had singled out for his counterpart', but as Mr Valiant-for-Truth, 'whom he had not hoped to emulate', and the chosen salute, the novel's closing lines, includes 'So he passed over, and all the trumpets sounded for him on the other side'. Buchan, incidentally, has already given us his version of predestination:

The enemy guns were starting to speak behind us, but I did not heed them. I knew that now there were warders at the gate, and I believed that by the grace of God that gate was barred for ever. (p.298)

As a novel of adventure *Mr Standfast* is a story of journeying – 'From the rocky coasts of Skye to a French château, from the Swiss mountains to the battlefields of the Western Front', to quote the blurb to the Pan edition – and the characters of the novel are all being tested by their adventures. We have seen that Buchan organizes this testing through consistent references to Bunyan's allegorical narrative, and so *Mr Standfast* proposes that the world of the war can be read in terms of the *Pilgrim's Progress*. Indeed, Bunyan's book is used as a code in a double sense: at the level of plot it unlocks mysteries, and at the moral and psychological level it decodes the complexities of the war situation. Moreover, Buchan's characters might well be seen as modelled on Bunyan's, for they are morality figures, incapable of significant change, development or surprise.

But – all this having been said – Buchan has learnt nothing of value from Bunyan: his response to *Pilgrim's Progress* is trivial. Bunyan writes spiritual autobiography as psychomachia, and he has the imagination to articulate the struggle of/for the soul in concrete terms, as well as the ability to break down the complexities of human moral nature without denying that this is complex. But Buchan operates in almost the opposite way. He starts with adventure in the sublunary world – the novelist's world of variety – and renders this with the simplifications of allegory, a process perfectly justifiable if it leads to illumination. In Bunyan simplification works to transmit the urgency of

[17]

Christian's search for salvation (or to discover if he is one of the elect) and, to convey how urgent this is for Everyman, Bunyan creates an externalized version of that spiritual search. Buchan, however, ends up with a simplification which constitutes an obscene reading of the war.

The continuous parallels with *Pilgrim's Progress*, especially in the second half of *Mr Standfast*, suggest that Hannay and his chums, representing 'us' at our finest, are travelling and fighting as Christian did. Hannay is Buchan's version of Christian, but it is significant that Hannay has almost nothing of Christian's doubts. Hannay can be passingly baffled by the complexities of the plot, but he is confident in his moral nature and values, whereas Christian has to struggle with his sense of his own weakness: salvation depends, for him, at least as much on this struggle as on any external obstacles between himself and the Heavenly City. This is a crucial difference. Bunyan's Christian makes sense as Everyman, while Buchan's Hannay is Christian as Superman.[3] Christian can still represent humanity, in its mixture of weakness and strength, whereas Hannay can only represent 'us', an élite viewed with breathtaking complacency.

If Hannay is Superman there can hardly be analysis of anything – certainly not of anything as complicated as the Great War and the societies which fought it out. As Superman, Hannay is simply right: his reactions are the correct ones, he is approved of and rewarded, his outlook reinforced by the other 'good' characters – by the representatives of Empire (white Empire – Pienaar), of Woman (Mary, of the significant name), of Empire's greatest offspring (the USA – Blenkiron) and by Authority at large. Germans are, 'by the grace of God', barred from the Heavenly City, and pacifists are shirkers (e.g. p. 30). In the *Pilgrim's Progress* the figures which differ from Christian represent aspects of his personality and he can only survive by resisting them and the threat they pose to his personality. The relationship between internal and external is more complex than this suggests, but the point is that even Apollyon and Despair participate in Christian's nature and are real dangers to his soul. Hannay's opponents do not touch him spiritually. They are not temptations so much as obstacles and he demonstrates his virtue and superiority by destroying them.

Hannay is a creative failure also on another level. Bunyan's hero seeks and achieves the Heavenly City: that is his goal and the urgency of his pilgrimage is conveyed in a way which gives the *Pilgrim's Progress* serious spiritual weight. In Buchan it is the sidekick, Pienaar, who 'passes over', and although we are to have no doubt that some vague Heavenly City awaits Hannay and his kind in an afterlife, we have equally no doubt that Hannay's satisfaction is to be in the here and now. He is to bask in the arms of Mary and in those of Tory Imperialism, while remaining ready to save the world (Anglo-Saxon civilization) from alien forces and influences.

So Hannay's pilgrimage is not really any more than the unravelling of the plot. Rather than a search for anything it is a demonstration of the superiority of Hannay and his like, and thus the parallels with Bunyan, so much insisted upon, are misleading, for Hannay's journeying is no true pilgrimage. Buchan learns nothing of human experience from Bunyan, mistaking the latter's strategic simplifications for his own simple-mindedness. This might not matter greatly if that simple-mindedness were genuinely innocent, but *Mr Standfast* is not a harmless book. It is dangerous because its simplifications reinforce prejudice. At best pacifism is seen with condescension as the aberration of the naïve; at best the non-British can only be granted full humanity by being made honorary Britons; at best Woman can be given full human status by being seen as boyish, a chum. So Pienaar is transformed into 'a soldier of Britain' and Mary into a boy. A deracinated South African white and a breastless, unsexed female, the one denied his racial integrity, the other her sexual, are the distorted figures which define the Buchan world. With its sublime unawareness of genuine thought and caring, its fundamental inhumanity, *Mr Standfast* not only insults Bunyan but represents exactly the kind of prejudice and racism which makes wars possible. The extent to which Buchan continues to be read with approval defines the extent to which we, like Buchan himself, have failed to learn either from *Pilgrim's Progress* or the Great War.

In his review of Henry Williamson's *The Patriot's Progress* in the *Evening Standard* Arnold Bennett said that 'John Bullock is Everysoldier, and *Everysoldier* would have been an excellent title for the book,' while T. E. Lawrence argued that 'The P. P. is natural man, making no great eyes at his sudden crisis.'[4] Williamson's central figure is unusual in English fiction dealing with the war in being a ranker,[5] a point made by the subtitle – 'Being the vicissitudes of Pte. John Bullock' – and his name is carefully chosen, echoing John Bull, as English Everyman (Bullock first hears of the Serbian crisis in the magazine *John Bull*) and John Ball (the medieval peasant leader and hero of William Morris's *A Dream of John Ball*). The surname also suggests the potency/potential of gonads, the latter association being marked in the bathing episode: 'Look at Nosey Bullock, crikey what a pair, 'is name shouldn't 'ave been Bullock, but . . .' (p. 79). And the initials are shared with John Bunyan.

Williamson does not offer detailed parallels with *Pilgrim's Progress*. His novel's title indicates that a parallel is intended, and where this leads is obvious enough. *The Patriot's Progress* is divided into 'phases' or significant episodes in Bullock's experience of the war, these being analogous to the main episodes of Christian's journey. Also, Bullock's progress is that of Everysoldier – enlistment, training, dispatch to the front; the 'luxury' of wash-house and brothel and drink. One of the things which anyone who reads novels of the Great War in bulk is made aware of is how limited the basic pattern is. The shape of a war largely defined by the trench imposed its own pattern on fiction, and even though there is infinite detail this is both rich and monotonous. Thus John Bullock's progress is an anthology of the expected, its pattern close to those of John Harris's late novel of the war, *Covenant with Death*, and Leon Wolff's non-fictional synthesis *In Flanders Fields* (1959; Penguin, 1979). Here again there is a parallel with Bunyan, for Christian's experience on his pilgrimage is that of any soul seeking salvation while Bullock's is that of any soldier under the war's pressure.

Bullock travels, makes a physical journey. In one sense his journey is circular, since he begins and ends in England. Something similar could be said of *Pilgrim's Progress,* in that Christian's journey, while linear, circles him back to his origin in God the Creator, but there is an important difference of emphasis. The major pull of Bunyan's book is linear, while that of Williamson's is centripetal. Christian moves from his domestic home in England to the Heavenly City, and, whatever his halts and doubts, he progresses and his journey is only circular in terms of an overview which sees it as a return to his true home. With Bullock the process is one whereby he is drawn into the war and then ejected from it, a piece of human flotsam. It is important to note here that Bullock enters the war as part of a mass. He makes no decision in any active (let alone epiphanic) sense, but responds to news and propaganda, to 'the common knowledge . . . in every newspaper, and on everyone's lips'. He enlists as part of a group: 'For hours John stood in a queue with other men . . . It was a nervous moment when, in a line with other men, he swore the Oath of Allegiance' (p. 7). A striking contrast follows from this difference of emphasis: Bunyan's linear pilgrimage is such that Christian's journeying is made significant by its goal, the Heavenly City, while Bullock's centripetal journey is imagined so that what his experience signifies is his destruction.

Bennett said that *The Patriot's Progress* 'is not a novel', and Lawrence claimed, in a letter to Williamson, that 'Tarka and this P. P. are better than your novels'.[6] The idea that *The Patriot's Progress* is not a novel links this book with other problematic fictions of the war (see Extended Notes, p. 142), but it also makes another connection with Bunyan. His *Pilgrim's Progress* occupies a curious place in the history of English fiction, influencing the development of the novel while remaining outside its chief areas of operation. Williamson, with his title claiming parallelism, implicitly suggests that his fiction is also not of the 'great tradition'. It is true that Bunyan's linear emphasis suggests the long tradition of novel-as-journey, but if one then links Christian and Christiana achieving the Heavenly City with, say, Tom and Sophia's journey to

[22]

marriage in *Tom Jones* it seems, by contrast, that Williamson's protagonist provides a version of the journey which allows only ironic progress.

In his preface Williamson does not explicitly deny that his book is a novel, but he quotes Bennett and Lawrence without disagreeing with them, and he tells us that the idea of *The Patriot's Progress* 'grew from a suggestion . . . that I should write captions for a set of lino-cuts which illustrated the Great War'. This developed into the idea of writing 'an entire story' around William Kermode's lino-cuts, 'pouring in a concrete of words making, as it were, a line of German mebus, or "pillboxes" of the kind which had frustrated our attacks during Third Ypres'. Kermode's lino-cuts would be 'shuttering to my verbal concrete'. The imagery is interesting: 'concrete', of course, suggests something which sets solid, and the pillbox analogy brings in the idea of objects to withstand the attacks of experience seen as flux and destruction. Something is to be *made* and the pillbox also acts as a memorial. But here again we have pilgrimage metamorphosed, for the pilgrimage is an image of purposive movement while the pillboxes of Bullock's experience seek to frustrate movement, replacing the dynamic impetus of the novel-as-journey with static blocks of memorialized experience. In one sense Williamson's structure *is* dynamic, with Bullock being drawn to destruction, but in another it is static, with the blocks being reminders of Everysoldier's essentially static experience, and thus, implicitly, the only memorial a Bullock can have. The pillboxes, products of the war, provide the proper memorials for those who died in it. This dynamic/static paradox applies also to Williamson's style, most clearly perhaps in 'Third Phase', which is a single block of prose, a paragraph of 38 pages. But the writing is at the same time dynamic, the style imploding in an attempt to render the simultaneity of multiple experience:

> Wheels rolled and jolted on. The hot-bodied foot-sloggers followed. Many halts. Curses. Brutal downward dronings of 5.9's. Ruddy flashes in front. Cra-ash. Cra-ash. Cra-ash. Cra-ash. John Bullock breathed faster. Cries came from far in front. Drivers crouched over their mules. For Christ's sake get a move on in front! They waited. The woo-r, woo-r, woo-r, plop, woo-r plop, of gas-shells, the corkscrewing downward sigh, the soft plop in the mud . . . (pp. 99–100)

Williamson uses Bunyan creatively but sardonically. Bunyan's pilgrim achieves the Heavenly City and the tribulations of his journey are seen to have value, its ending being in salvation. In Williamson's version the patriot–pilgrim journeys to the front and back home, but the Heavenly City remains elusive, replaced by the England which greets the returning Bullock. The linear aspect of *The Patriot's Progress* has its terminus at the front, which is by analogy equivalent to the Heavenly City, but heaven is now hell. For the path to the Heavenly City we are led to substitute the inward-leading circles of Dante's hell. Yet Bullock, drawn to the centre of the circle, is then rejected, thrown back whence he came and this is an ironic salvation. The path which led to the front also leads from it and this allows for the possibility of another Heavenly City – home. But home is a wasteland for Bullock. The 'toff' of the book's last moments rebukes a small boy: 'This good man is a hero,' and he goes on to address Bullock: 'Yes . . . we'll see that England doesn't forget you fellows,' to which Bullock replies: 'We are England.' The Bullock who speaks is disabled and unemployed. Instead of a traveller reaching the Heavenly City he has been destroyed by his pilgrimage, is a wanderer or lost soul.

2. The Great War and crucifixion

Bunyan's pattern helped Williamson to make sense of the war, but he achieves this by ironizing *Pilgrim's Progress*. There was, however, another journey which might have helped novelists to see pattern and purpose in the war – the journey of Christ to crucifixion and beyond, a journey both to the death of a common criminal and to the provision of new hope for humanity in Christ's refusal to despair, as this is manifested in the resurrection and ascension.

Crucifixion, though only one of the ways in which humanity shows its inhumanity, has a special status in the eyes of believers, because Christ's execution is blasphemy and because that act can be seen as a collective human suicide. The idea of the Christ-killer is an obvious one for propaganda and British propaganda made full use of the idea that this was the German role in the war. Moreover, the crucifixion may have made a particular impression on British soldiers because of the ubiquity of crucifixes in Belgium and France, for these soldiers were (at least nominally) Protestants operating in Catholic territory.

Perhaps the most famous piece of war propaganda was that of 'the crucified Canadian',[7] in which the soldier is identified with Christ, and such identification occurs also at this moment in Frederic Manning's novel *Her Privates We*:[8]

> They marched out of the village, past the stone calvary at the end of it, and men who had known all the sins of the world lifted, to the agony of the figure on the cross, eyes

that had probed and understood the mystery of suffering.
(p. 129)

This moment is preceded by Bourne's reflections on
Colonel Bardon's inspection. Bardon's face is severe,
'just, merciless', his eyes 'incisive'. He passes 'like some
impersonal force'. Bardon is seen in terms of 'reciprocal
obligations': he is necessary in the context of the war,
but the necessities of command entail 'a great deal of
reserve' (pp. 161–2). When the soldiers march out,
however, their eyes look elsewhere, at the 'agony of the
figure on the cross', and the suggestion is that there is
mutual empathy, from which comes the sense that the
soldiers are themselves Christs, experiencing the mystery of the crucifixion. Manning's novel does not make
this association explicit as a reading of the war. He does
not, that is, make his soldiers into Christ figures who,
in the orthodox Christian sense, suffer to redeem
mankind, but he does see the suffering of war as
redemptive. His hero, Bourne, achieves a serenity
through experience, and this serenity includes a
necessary mystery about understanding such experience. So Sergeant Tozer accepts Bourne's death 'with a
quiet fatalism', 'with a quiet acceptance of the fact', and
reflects that 'there's a bit of a mystery about all of us';
while Manning presents the death with a Christ-echo:
'It was finished' (p. 301). But Manning provides no
resurrection. His book ends in uncertainty, with each
survivor 'keeping his own secret' (p. 302), and in so far
as the death of Bourne has Christian implications these
are held at the level of possibilities rather than
certainties. Orthodox Christianity comprehends the
crucifixion through the resurrection and the promise of
eternal life, but in Manning these remain unknowable.
Yet Christ's journey to the cross and beyond has clearly

been used as a motif which helps Bourne to find peace even in the midst of appalling experiences.[9] How sustaining the pattern is here is obvious if it is compared with a much later version of Christ crucified, that in Harris's *Covenant with Death*. There the aftermath of battle 'was like being in the graveyard of civilization', or 'like a Gustave Doré etching of Purgatory'. In this scene 'From the bent iron calvary nearby, Jesus Christ stared down on them with iron unfeeling eyes and iron cheeks' (pp. 369–70).

Ernest Raymond, in *Tell England* (Cassell, 1922; the quotations are from pp. 316–7), offers neither Manning's limited identification of the soldier with crucifixion nor Harris's use of the cross as icon of alienation and despair. For Raymond the crucifixion is a simple source of comfort. At the end of his novel he writes of the sermon preached by Monty ('an old Peninsula padre') at the 'unveiling of a memorial in the chapel to the Old Kensingtonians who fell at Gallipoli'. The chaplain describes Calvary as 'a sacrifice offered by a Holy Family', this of course being God the Father, Mary and Christ the Son. And he goes on to say that 'in days to come, England must remember that once upon a time she, too, was a Holy Family', this consisting of the English mothers and fathers who 'gave their sons', and of the sons themselves, who are presented as reflecting the words 'It was written of me that I should do Thy will; I am content to do it' (see, for example, *Luke* 22:42 and *Matthew* 26:42). We are a long way here from responses like Sassoon's bitter attacks on home. This is a unified England, but also an England so clearly God's country as to be a replica of the Holy Family. But it is also an England of Buchan's kind. The particular son of whom the padre is thinking is 'That boy, an old Kensingtonian' and although it would, perhaps, be unfair to suggest that Raymond is consciously excluding rankers and their families from his England it is evident that his idea of England is the Christ-like public-school officer, with his parents the God and Blessed Virgin of club and country house. Raymond, it seems, finds nothing disturbing in seeing the war in terms of Christ's journey to crucifixion. God is an Englishman of the propertied middle class, and we are offered a highly comforting, conservative and complacent transformation of the Jewish carpenter.

Raymond uses a padre to present this vision, and a padre is the central figure of C. R. Bensted's *Retreat* (Methuen, 1930). Yet of the two authors, it was Raymond who was a padre and Raymond who seems to have suffered more from the war, renouncing Holy Orders after it, which gives *Tell England* a certain pathos. Bensted's padre, Warne, is, however, not a veteran but a priest on active service, and his parishioners see him as the church's militant representative at the front. Thus, the butcher's wife writes that 'We are proud to think of our Rector out there in the thick of it, holding up the Cross of Jesus before our boys' (p. 225). Warne attempts to fulfil this role. He comes to the war naïve and uncertain, and early in the novel he lies asleep in his billet, with his 'little ivory cross rising on its plinth of ebony from the litter of a bachelor's dressing-table'. But although Warne is asleep 'he was not entirely at rest, inert though his body lay, for imagination insisted upon working that ivory cross into strange and disturbing fantasy, and linking it with visions of that other Cross which stood on Calvary' (pp. 36–7). In a sense this summarizes the whole novel, in which Warne tries to accommodate the neat inexperience of his priestly life at home to the Golgotha of the front.

Retreat is a forgotten and rather clumsy novel, but it conveys a sense of integrity which is finally quite impressive. Bensted has a strong feeling for orthodox religion and a reader's expectation is that the basic social and religious orthodoxy of the novel will lead, however improbably – given Warne's personality – to his success and thus the triumph of the way of the cross. Warne sees himself as an outsider, functionless in a world of highly professional men, and he quests throughout for a role which will justify him as man and priest. Intermittently he feels he has found such a role, as here:

> To Warne, in surplice and stole, his cassock over his khaki uniform, it seemed that God Himself had suddenly stepped into the barn, and was bidding him be of good cheer, so that for the moment all the doubts of the last month fell away, leaving him as he had been in the prime of his Faith . . . (p. 269)

But this *is* only intermittent, and the novel's strength lies in its honesty. Warne does finally act with heroism, when, despite his almost catatonic state, he forces himself, 'quivering in a palsy of terror' (p. 302), to help Cheyne rescue men trapped by bombardment. This seems to be Warne's redemption after the prolonged crucifixion of his war, and Cheyne and O'Reilly recognize the achievement:

> Nodding after him, O'Reilly remarked: 'There's some of the Faith that moves mountains in him. But – '
> Cheyne laughed, a nervous, effervescing sort of thing. 'I wish to God I had a little. A man in his state who can force himself . . .' (p. 303)

But it is a wry redemption. Raymond's padre dies of 'nervous exhaustion': Warne goes mad. In his breakdown he parts company with his faith:

[29]

> Only the jagged ruins of the Church awoke any reaction
> in his consciousness, and that he beheld with a sort of
> bewildered protesting sense of personal loss.

And

> Unbridled at last, his voice rose to the frenzied scream he
> had so long feared. And thus he denied his God. (pp. 309,
> 311)

The apostate Warne dies in June 1918, victim of the
war 'that had crushed his spirit and killed his soul'
(p. 317). Therefore the quotation on the 'tablet in the
Church at Bidderwill' – 'Greater love hath no man
than this' – is both grimly inappropriate and fitting
(p. 318). Bensted's novel does not reject Christianity,
for O'Reilly and Cheyne speak of mutation, but it sees
the war as crushing the traditional version which
Warne has represented. If Christianity is to survive it
must change: the crucifixion of Christ failed to sustain
Warne or to provide Bensted with a consoling pattern.

3. The Great War and sport

For British novelists, perhaps more than for others,
there was a third image, or set of images, which offered
a pattern by which the war might be read. I am
thinking of sport, with its various suggestive links with
war. Some sports are directly connected with military
training, while the major contact sports share with war
the concept of controlled aggression to obtain victory.
Moreover, sport is defined by rules which say what is
and is not permissible, these rules merging with tacit
codes of behaviour found in expressions such as 'That's
not cricket' and 'Playing the game'. Sport also involves
the definition of the playing space and the specification
of equipment.

[30]

Much of this also applies to war. Efforts to conduct warfare by rules are very old (and were a feature of the 1907 Peace Conference at The Hague) while the whole concept of chivalry, at least in its mature form, has much in common with the idea of the spirit of the game, even to the extent of mitigating the degree to which mutilation and death are acceptable outcomes of war. Further the 'rules of war' include efforts to define its equipment (thus, for example, the pre-First World War agreements on gas and aircraft).[10] Codification and definition apply to both areas of experience, while training, in the sense of developing specific skills and fitness, and also in the self-discipline of accepting and responding positively to corporate discipline, is fundamental to both. In both areas victory is understood to depend on training in its various senses.

So it is not difficult to see why war and sport are often used as images for each other, or why sports training and competition play an important part in military institutions. But it is important to be aware that it is dangerous to think of war in terms of sport. Thought of in that way war becomes socialized, its world comprehended in terms of an activity which society actively encourages. Seen in terms of accepted rules war itself becomes acceptable. But war's *raison d'être* is domination and its mode is destruction. Getting a bullet in the brain is *not* like losing your leg stump; bombing Dresden is *not* like scoring the winning goal at Wembley; occupying and holding an enemy salient is *not* like 'camping out' on your opponents' 25 at Twickenham. Beyond this, there is the more immediately relevant fact that the First World War restated war's basic anarchy: the traditional codifications, whether of rule or of spirit, break down so that ideas of war as defined, and thus capable of being seen whole, as from grandstand or terrace, collapse as the war continues. This is evident both in explicit statements by combatants and in the strong tendency of literature of this war to fragment, communicating the sense that significant expression precludes overview.

Yet the literature of the Great War makes frequent use of sporting analogies and it seems particularly common among British writers. The obvious reason for this is that many sports seem to have originated in Britain. It was also perhaps easier for the British to see war as sport since direct experience of the former was so limited between the Civil War and the Blitz. War was something which happened elsewhere and, being filtered by distance, was the more easily reduced to the terminology of sport. Finally, the tendency in the so-called 'public' schools of the nineteenth century to see education as primarily training for public service led to an emphasis on team sports as being appropriate to such training. The domination by the ex-pupils of fee-paying schools of positions of prestige and power meant that attitudes defined in such schools filtered down to other social levels.

Kipling's George Cottar, in the pre-war story 'The Brushwood Boy', is a fine example of how this sort of training might be related to the military life. Cottar's school 'was not encouraged to dwell on its emotions, but rather to keep in hard condition, to avoid false quantities, and to enter the army direct' (*The Day's Work* (1898), Macmillan, 1964. The quotations are from pp. 288, 292, 299–300). Kipling presents Cottar's career as a continuous progression from school to army and Cottar sees the latter in terms of the former:

. . . he did not forget that the difference between a dazed and sulky junior of the upper school and a bewildered, browbeaten lump of a private fresh from the depot was very small indeed.

Cottar's men are his successes:

> ... they were good children in camp ... and they followed their officers with the quick suppleness and trained obedience of a first-class football fifteen.

In this world life is reduced to the rugby pack and is then understood in terms of conformity to, or divergence from, this ideal. Kipling's example is particularly strong in War novels meant for boys, as in Herbert Strang's *Fighting with French* when, at a crisis involving three spies and the hero, Kenneth, 'the years of training on the football field, in the gymnasium, on Mr Kishimaru's practice lawn, bore fruit in instantaneous decision and rapid action' (Frowde, 1915, p. 189) – and the greatest of these is rugby, for Kenneth stooped, 'tackled the nearest of the other men, and brought him down' (p. 189). In such cases there is no emphasis on officer training within the army: it seems as though, for such young men, school provides all that is necessary.

War seen as sport can be presented in terms of 'play', as it is in Wells's *Mr Britling Sees It Through* ((1916), Waterlow, 1933, p. 201) when Britling's son Hugh says '. . . I begin to perceive that war is absolutely the best game in the world . . . you have all the world to play with, and you may use whatever you can use'. Hugh Britling, however, comes to know better in a novel which comes to know better. But more usually the references to war as game carry the Victorian and Edwardian view of life as a game to be played, not with instinctive joy, but with the pleasures of duty and discipline – 'with the quick suppleness and trained obedience of a first-class football fifteen'. This is what is

[33]

going on when Buchan's Hannay is being prepared for another adventure by Sir Walter Bullivant of the Foreign Office. Bullivant tells Hannay that this 'is a wonderful war for youth and brains . . . It is a great game, and you are the man for it, no doubt' (*Greenmantle* (1916), Penguin, 1956, p. 15). Gilbert Fraukau's Peter Jackson, a volunteer waiting to go to France, 'felt the uplift of the game' (*Peter Jackson: Cigar Merchant,* Hutchinson, 1920, p. 132), and Jackson, like Hannay, thinks of life as serving your country. Or the game becomes a mystery and the war is then something whose rules are learnt and accepted because games are valuable. Bensted's Warne is a good example:

> And they, on their side, noted a travel-stained and pathetically earnest priest, obviously new to the game he was going to play, and it occurred to both the Colonel and Cheyne that he knew precious little of what the game involved. (*Retreat* p. 20)

Warne, of course, never fully learns, is never an initiate of the game, and goes mad.

Such a view of the game draws in rankers as well as officers, and the mysterious worth of the game is made explicit in 'Sapper's' story 'The Land of Topsy Turvy', when the colonel addresses the regiment on the subject of 'sticking it':

> 'Stick it, my lads . . . Stick it, for the credit of the regiment, for the glory of our name . . . Each one of us counts, men' – his voice sank a little – 'each one of us has to play the game. Not because we're afraid of being punished if we're found out, but because it *is* the game.' (*Men, Women and Guns,* Hodder and Stoughton, 1916, p. 264)

[34]

This is, of course, an appeal to the spirit of the game, and its language reduces being shot for desertion to the punishments of the school system.

'Sapper's' colonel shifts the emphasis from the formal rules of the game to playing it in the correct spirit. Learning the rules and conforming to them is not enough: they need to be complemented by identification with the values of the game. Kipling's Cottar embodies 'playing the game' and the view recurs in war fiction. Peter Jackson, for example, tells his wife of his decision to join up:

> 'Pat,' he began, 'I don't think I can keep out of this thing any longer. It wouldn't be' – he fumbled for the expression – 'quite playing the game . . .' (p. 62)

And, in *Retreat,* Dalgith's momentary feeling of guilt over Warne is 'as if, in some obscure way, he had been guilty of not playing the game and had been found out' (p. 179). But the phrase is not one which is much used by those writers who seem fully aware of the pressure the war put on such sporting ideas. The spirit of war as game could not easily survive in thinking minds.

Yet although the idea of playing the game does not provide much of a framework for war fiction, the prominence of sport in British society is nevertheless seen on the many occasions when writers define aspects of war experience in sporting terms. So Cecil Lewis talks of 'miraculous' survival in the air: '. . . as time went by and left you unscathed, like a batsman who has played himself in, you began to take liberties with the bowling' (*Sagittarius Rising* (1936), Penguin, 1977, p. 56. Lewis's book is one of those which live on the borders of novel and memoir). Ernest Raymond has a similar image: '. . . from all I knew of Doe and his passion for the heroic, I felt assured that he would

[35]

never stay in the crater like a diffident batsman in his block. He would reach the opposite crease, or be run out.' Doe is 'run out' and at the moment of his death 'the wind blew his hair about, as it used to do on the cricket-field at school' (pp. 287, 290). The image here is genuinely pathetic, for this young officer dies very close to his schooldays. But the image of the reckless batsman perhaps reveals more than the writers realize, for the batsman who charges the bowler gives him extra chances and this is hardly good thinking in a war. It remains true, however, that such usages do provide an example of how images from pre-war can be used to suggest something of war experience, in this case the innocence of the initiate.

Predictably enough, the sporting images tend to come from the activities of the privileged. Frankau's Jackson finds that his work as battery subaltern provides the thrill of bursting his shell exactly in the enemy's face, a sensation 'only to be compared with tiger-shooting from an elephant's howdah' (p. 287), while, later in the novel, an exhausting journey from Trones Wood is ' "Like rowing," he thought, "got to put your last ounce into it"; and like a rowed-out oarsman he rested for a little . . .' (p. 307). But it is Lord Dunsany who perhaps shows most clearly how war-as-sport can be a fatuous transformation:

We come presently to the dens of those who trouble us, but only for our own good – the dug-outs of the trench mortar batteries. It is noisy when they push up close to the front line and play for half an hour or so with their rivals. The enemy sends stuff back; our artillery join in. It is as though, while you were playing a game of croquet, giants hundreds of feet high, some of them friendly, some unfriendly, carnivorous and hungry, came and played football on your croquet lawn. (*Tales of War*, Fisher Unwin, 1918, pp. 36–7)

[36]

The noise, squalor and danger are rendered Carroll-like, but with nothing of Carroll's psychological edge – and the game in question is slightly comic, a minor pastime of the genteel, threatened by ruffians who play football.

By Dunsany's standards 'Ian Hay' is a model of sensitivity and perception. Paul Fussell says that *The First Hundred Thousand* shows 'how much wholesome fun is to be had at the training camp' and that the book 'is really very good, nicely written and thoroughly likable' (p. 28). But when 'Hay' concentrates on trench experience in *Carrying On – After the First Hundred Thousand* his basically facetious manner serves only to deflect and distort, with sporting allusions working to conceal truth rather than analyse it. So chapter 3 is called 'Winter Sports: Various' (with tunnelling as 'a very pretty game of subterranean chess'; Blackwood, 1917, p. 68) while among those who play in an inter-brigade game of Rugby Union are officers 'whose last game had been one of the spring "Internationals" of 1914, and who had been engaged in a prolonged and strenuous version of an even greater International ever since August of that fateful year' (p. 111) – where the key words are 'even greater' and where the analogy again claims a continuum from playing field to battlefield. Late in the novel we come to golf. Asked by Major Wagstaff how 'consolidation' is going Angus M'Lachlan replies, 'We have won the match, sir . . . We are just playing the bye now!', and, for Wagstaff, that is M'Lachlan's epitaph:

> You remember his remark to me, that we only had the bye to play now? He was a true prophet: we are dormy, anyhow. (pp. 271, 315)

Elsewhere such efforts to reduce aspects of the war to such comfortable terms are replaced by more sensitive treatment which, for example, says something about the

tensions of waiting to go into action. Lewis uses
running for early experience of flying – 'God! Who said
they wanted to fly? How the heart pumps! Waiting for
the pistol at the school races last year! Just the same –
sick, heart pumping, no breath . . .' (*Sagittarius Rising*,
p. 24). Ernest Raymond has Rupert inspecting his
company, his restlessness bringing back 'vividly that
day when I had suffered from nerves before the
Bramhall–Erasmus swimming race. The same interior
hollowness made me chafe at delay and long to be
started' (*Tell England*, p. 286).

It is striking in these cases that the images work,
because they are the natural images of young patricians still essentially innocent of the war, as of life at
large. Since their experience is largely of school they
can, as yet, think only in terms of school. Lewis is
intelligent enough in his book to get beyond his
sporting images as innocence gives way to experience,
and it can be claimed that he uses such images to define
immaturity, thus showing some sense that the analogy
between war and sport has severe limitations. Neither
Dunsany nor 'Hay' gets this far.

But when, in the fiction of the war, the idea of war as
sport breaks down, the collapse comes in some rather
strange forms, as in 'Sapper's' 'The Land of Topsy
Turvy'. There the doctor is outraged at some German
prisoners ('those swine – all toddling off to Donington
Hall – happy as you like'), contrasting their treatment
with that of Allied troops in German hands, who are
'Stuck with bayonets, hit, brutally treated, half-starved,
thrown into cattle trucks'. Jim tries to restrain the
doctor: 'We're not the sort to go in for retribution . . .
After all – oh! I don't know – but it's not quite cricket,
is it? Just because they're swine . . . ?' But the doctor is
only the more angry:

[38]

> Cricket! . . . You make me tired. I tell you I'm sick to
> death of our kid-glove methods. No retribution! I suppose
> if a buck nigger hit your pal over the head with a club
> you'd give him a tract on charity and meekness. (pp.
> 294–5)

In this exchange the spirit of sport is seen by the doctor
as inadequate because the enemy is not, to his mind,
'playing the game'. 'Frightfulness' can only be dealt
with by counter-frightfulness, and the doctor invokes
comradeship and race hatred to bolster his case, one
which is sadly similar to the arguments of modern
advocates of nuclear 'deterrents'.

In *Winged Victory* V. M. Yeates gets slightly beyond
this, although his critique only questions the validity of
sporting images for *this* war. Tom reflects on 'How life
had changed in the last four days!' Here very recent
experience has transformed marginally less recent
experience, when flying jobs were 'gentlemanly affairs
at stated times, with regular days off and plenty of dud
weather'. But

> That was all far away; and now the flowering of the
> cavalry and cricket mind of the professional soldier was
> being seen. They had never been able to regard trench
> warfare as real war; where were the horses and the
> lances?

Such views 'would have won the war long ago if the
Germans had played the game. But they didn't; they
had Hindenberg lines and no traditions . . .' ((1934),
Mayflower, 1974, p. 110)

War-as-sport is here seen as having been made into
an anachronism by the Germans, but Tom's tone
contains nothing of the self-righteousness of 'Sapper's'
doctor. It is itself professional, detached, ironical, but it
seems only to want the updating of the imagery and

[39]

does not press very hard on what the war/sport comparisons involve. Ford Madox Ford, offering what seems a similar account, goes beyond Yeates at this moment in *Parade's End*. His protagonist, Tietjens, in one of Ford's many passages which mix direct and indirect speech, tells Captain Mackenzie that 'The curse of the army, as far as the organization is concerned, was our imbecile national belief that the game is more than the player . . . We were taught that cricket is more than clearness of mind, so the blasted quartermaster . . . thought he had taken a wicket if he refused to serve out tin hats to their crowd . . . And if any of his, Tietjens', men were killed, he grinned and said the game was more than the players of the game . . .' Mackenzie demurs: 'Oh, damn it! . . . That's what made us what we are, isn't it?', to which Tietjens replies: 'It is! . . . It's got us into the hole and it keeps us there.' (This is from *No More Parades* (1925), which is the second volume of the *Parade's End* trilogy; Sphere, 1969, p. 20.) Caught up in the war as he is, Tietjens shows concern for the 'players' as many subalterns did, but he also sees that war-as-sport encourages the taming of war and is properly uneasy about the implications of this.[11]

This chapter has tried to indicate something of how difficult it was for novelists to use such patterns as the ones discussed without betraying their material or making considerable adaptations. Comparisons between war and sport depend upon acceptance that the two areas of experience have enough genuinely in common for comparisons to be illuminating. This was not the case in the First World War, except within very narrow limits, and so the only analytically useful comparisons are ironic, suggesting something about the war by indicating that sporting images will not do. Something similar might be said of attempts to compare the war with pilgrimage or with Christ's journey to the cross. Here the difficulty is that both of these are, for believers, journeys of hope. Christian reaches the Heavenly City; Christ's crucifixion is followed by resurrection, ascension and the harrowing of hell. The war put such pressure on belief that, at the least, orthodox Christianity needed re-examination. Among the novelists, failure to attempt this led, as with Buchan and Raymond, to uses of these patterns which are of little value as analysis of the war, although they are obliquely most revealing. When re-examination is attempted, as with Williamson and Bensted, the patterns are read ironically.

What this suggests is obvious enough; that such patterns as those looked at in this chapter, patterns formed in history before the war, were put under acute pressure by war experience. Another way of saying the same thing would be to comment that the Great War was a deeply transformative experience. The next chapter will look more closely at this view.

II

Richard Aldington and Transformation

In *A Diary without Dates* Enid Bagnold writes of a man
she calls Gayner, who has been wounded at Mons. He is
asked, as he lies in hospital, 'Don't you ever read?' and
answers 'I haven't the patience.' Bagnold comments:

> But he has the patience to lie like that with his thin lips
> compressed and a frown on his face for hours, for days . . .
> since Mons . . . ((1918) Virago, 1978, pp. 95–6)

Gayner's wound, it seems, has obliterated him, or at
least driven him in upon himself, away from contact.
Bagnold also tells of Waker who, like Gayner, is altered
by an 'accident of war' which changed his whole career.
From 'that moment football was off, and with it his
particular ambition' (p. 122).

These are very specific moments and might be
contrasted with the broad reflective sweep of Philip
Gibbs in 1924:

> Old habits of thought have been smashed; old securities,
> traditions, obediences, convictions, lie in wreckage and,
> unlike the ruins of the war itself, will never be restored.
> We are different men and women. (*Ten Years After*,
> Hutchinson, p. 8)

Here the effort to summarize has led to the language of
apocalypse – 'smashed . . . wreckage . . . ruins'.

[42]

It would be easy enough to fill the gap between Bagnold's details and Gibbs's generalizations, but the point I want to make is simply that both writers touch one of the most important ways of seeing the First World War — as transformation, even apocalypse. This is an approach which has its positive version at the outbreak of the war with the image of war as a cleansing agent, most famously in Rupert Brooke's sonnet, 'Peace'. But although some later writers also feel able to make something positive from the war's destruction (notably Cecil Lewis in his introduction to *Sagittarius Rising* (1936) and Guy Chapman in *A Kind of Survivor* (1975)), the epiphanies of this war are mainly negative. The war breaks people and things, makes pre-war into instant history. So the author of the story 'All Our Yesterdays' speaks of 'tokens of the world I used to know', and David Jones tells of recruits being given lectures 'redolent of a vanished order'. (*Short Stories of the First World War*, ed. G. Bruce, Sidgwick and Jackson, 1971, p. 47; *In Parenthesis* (1937), Faber, 1963, p. 13)

The novelist of the war stands somewhere between the diarist and the writer of an official military history. On the one hand the novelist needs the detail of the diarist, but on the other has a concern with larger units of shape than usually concern the writer of a diary. Richard Aldington is the novelist who is most preoccupied with the idea of the war as transforming its victims and he works hard to find a pattern to embody this preoccupation, most famously in his first novel, *Death of a Hero* (1929).

On p. 198 of my text (Consul edition, 1965) Aldington begins one of his frequent passages of authorial commentary, asking of the Great War 'Why did it happen?

Who was responsible?' But, he says, for those of his generation, the generation of the war, 'the debate is vain, as vain as the pathetic and reiterated inquiry. "*Where* did I catch this horrible cold?"' Yet he is in no doubt about the scale of the event, a 'catastrophe', a 'shattering success', and goes on:

> Adult lives were cut sharply into three sections – pre-war, war, and post-war. It is curious . . . but many people will tell you that whole areas of their pre-war lives have become obliterated from their memories. Pre-war seems like pre-history . . . One feels as if the period 1900–14 has to be treated archaeologically, painfully restored by experts from slight vestiges.

The language of surgery and obliteration, of archaeology and recreation is intimate with that of transformation: that which was no longer is; that which is is not what was. It matters less whether or not Aldington, looking back from the late twenties, was right to see 1914–18 as a period of transformation, than that he thought of it in this way. But it is important, at once, to make the point that the idea of transformation is more than a matter of passing authorial comment: it is central to the conception and structure of *Death of a Hero*.

The novel is basically an account of how George Winterbourne was so acted upon as to commit a form of suicide almost at the war's end. And although Aldington does not claim that all soldiers are driven so far, he does claim that George's transformation is typical in its pattern:

> He had reached the first expressionless stage of the war soldier, which is followed by the period of acute strain; and that in turn gives place to the second expressionless stage – which is pretty hopeless. (p. 238)

[44]

Suicide is, for Winterbourne, only literalization of the 'second expressionless stage'. Aldington confidently represents his hero as typical, and confidently anatomizes a soldier's 'progress' in war.

But it is not only the soldier himself who is changed; his change necessitates transformation in his relationships with those not directly involved in the fighting. George had apparently gone to the war as a reasonably well-adjusted young man, some way into coping with the traumas of his upbringing, and this coping had involved, most importantly, what Aldington ironically calls 'the Triumphal Scheme for the Perfect Sex Relation' (p. 226). But, as the war closes on George, Elizabeth and Fanny both take on greater significance for him and also fail to live up to this. In the special circumstances of the war 'they had acquired a sort of mythical and symbolical meaning for him ... they represented what hope of humanity he had left; in them alone civilization seemed to survive.' One of the bigger ironies of the novel is that George places the 'hope of humanity' where he does, but the important point here is that he sees his women as the only source of hope – 'All the rest was blood and brutality and persecution and humbug.' Yet 'Unfortunately, they did not ... perceive the widening gulf which was separating the men of that generation from the women. How could they? The friends of a person with cancer haven't got cancer ... aren't in the horrid category of the doomed' (p. 227). The imagery of gulfs, cancer and doom is commonplace in the literature of the war, but our sense of how much the split means to George is increased when we remember Aldington's constant effort to indicate how isolated his generation feels.

Any such vision of radical transformation must put considerable stress on a writer's sense of form and style. John Johnston has argued (*English Poetry of the First World War,* Oxford, 1964, *passim*) that the extraordinary conditions and pressures of the war experience made it almost inevitable that lyric would be the dominant literary form of the war period itself (with, I suppose, letters and diaries as the sub-literary equivalent). Such a thesis at least serves to remind us that – except for Barbusse's *Le Feu* and Bennett's *The Pretty Lady* – the major fiction of the Great War does not begin to emerge until some years after its end: *Kangaroo* in 1923, Ford's *Some Do Not* in 1924; Remarque's *All Quiet* . . . in 1929, Manning's *Her Privates We* in 1930. This lapse of time is of interest here as a symbol of the pressures on form and style: how do I write adequately of such an enormity? What lessons of the literary past can apply to that experience? Aldington himself was aware of the problems. In his autobiography he tells us that he made three abortive attempts at a novel about his war experience before he was able to write *Death of a Hero* (*Life for Life's Sake,* Cassell, 1941, p. 301).[1]

Not surprisingly different writers found different solutions to such problems. David Jones, mixing prose and verse, tries to find formal anchorage in myth. Barbusse and Remarque both largely abandon the convention of the central hero in favour of concentration on the representative group (a choice which is for Barbusse as much political as aesthetic) while Henry Williamson, in *The Patriot's Progress,* creates a hero intended, as the title suggests, to be representative of the ranker-at-large. What George represents, however, is the product of specific temporal and spatial shapings: *Death of a Hero* is sociological in emphasis rather than philosophical.

As we shall see, Aldington's rather scornful attitude to form is part of the generally cynical voice of his novel. In the dedication to his friend, the dramatist Halcott

Glover, he says that 'This book is not the work of a professional novelist. It is, apparently, not a novel at all . . . To me the excuse for the novel is that one can do any damn thing one pleases . . .' This is the voice of the no-nonsense amateur: 'I don't know anything about Art, but I know what I like' (Anon.); 'I knew what I wanted to say, and said it' (Aldington, dedication). There are, it seems, no problems of form: you simply say what you want to say. But Aldington is being disingenuous, for his novel is neither formless nor unconcerned with form, despite the remarks just quoted and the throwaway line 'I suppose this is a jazz novel.'

In the first place, Aldington's title suggests a controlling purpose, one quickly registered as doubly ironic. The heroic tradition of warfare is obviously gestured at in the title, and is underlined by the prologue's sub-title, where 'Morte d'un Eroë' indicates the Arthurian literary tradition. The double irony, of course, is that George Winterbourne is, by such standards, no hero at all – but the standards, Aldington's novel asserts, no longer apply, and the memorialization of George is an assertion that he *is* a hero, of the new dispensation. But the formal control suggested by the heroic reference does not work out as a governing principle for the novel, remaining only part of the book's intermittent allusiveness.

A more helpful sign of the formal concern in the making of *Death of a Hero* is the musical terminology which provides the headings for the book's sections – allegretto, vivace, andante cantabile, adagio. In *Life for Life's Sake* Aldington says 'I wanted the writing to give the effect of the different movements of a symphony' (p. 302). This indicates several things – a search for some form which will be adequate for an account of war experience; a formal concern which contradicts the casualness indicated above; and perhaps a desire to imitate Lawrence's use of structures which represent phases of experience rather than the traditional serial chapters. Aldington's use of section and sub-section suggests a structure of motif and modulation, rather than the progressive norm of the 'traditional novel', and indicates the effort of reflection.[2]

Yet what Aldington says in his dedication agrees with what he does in his novel in so far as he turns away from the orthodox narrative line of the middle-brow professional novelist. The dedication suggests, with typical arrogant diffidence, that this is because the author is just an amateur with something to say (a gifted public-school cricketer whose livelihood has nothing to do with net practice). But Aldington is bluffing, and his methods are a serious artistic effort to find due form for fictional satire of the elements which shape and define war. This effort inevitably also defines the novel's style.

Clearly, anyone who writes about the Great War and who has a sense of that war as something which transformed the nations and individuals taking part in it will be aware, at some level of consciousness, that the words he uses are themselves liable to be transformed. What, for instance, does the word 'hero' mean by 1918? Or the word 'patriot'? What happened, within the war, to the sanctity of the idea of individual conscience?

Two particular results occur when words are under acute pressure. One is that individual words no longer seem able adequately to stand for their 'objects', with the result that the word-user is drawn to repetition, or to paradox ('honourable murderer', *Death of a Hero*, p. 222) or to litotes ('the jumps' to refer to Winterbourne's breakdown, p. 191). The other result of such pressure is that the writer's linguistic register tends to work towards fragmentation, the writing becoming

[48]

abrupt, with sharp variations of register, jerky trans-
missions, and even hectic inventiveness – these all
reducing the possibilities of coherence and increasing
the chances of uncertainties of tone and stance.[3]

Until its final part, Aldington's novel has a dominant,
binding satirical style, designed to convey his 'loathing
and contempt' for Victorian and Edwardian values and
viewpoints. It is usually a rather heavy satire, with
points strongly marked by repetition, ironic juxtaposition, authorial comment and emphatic underlining, all
of which are present in this passage, the account of the
reception by his mother of the news of George's death:

In low moaning tones, founded on the best tradition of
sensational fiction, Mrs Winterbourne feebly ejaculated:
  'Dead, dead, dead!'
  'Who's dead? Winterbourne?'
  (Some apprehension perhaps in the attendant Sam
Browne – he would have to propose, of course, and might
be accepted.)
  'They've killed him, those vile *filthy* foreigners. My
baby son.'
  Sam Browne, still mystified, read the telegram. He
then stood to attention, saluted (although not wearing a
cap), and said solemnly:
  'A clean sportin' death, an *Englishman's* death.'
  (When Huns were killed it was neither clean nor
sportin', but served the beggars – ('buggers', among
men) sob – right.)
  The tears Mrs Winterbourne shed were not very
natural, but they did not take long to dry. Dramatically,
she ran to the telephone. Dramatically, she called to the
local exchange:
  'Trrrunks. (Sob.) Give me Kensington 1030. Mr Winterbourne's number, you know. (Sob). Our *darling* son –
Captain Winterbourne – has been killed by those (Sob)
beasts. (Sob. Pause.) Oh, thank you *so* much, Mr Crump,

I *knew* you would feel for us in our trouble. (Sob. Sob.)
But the blow is so sudden. I *must* speak to Mr Winter-
bourne. Our hearts are *breaking* here. (Sobissimo.)
Thank you. I'll wait till you ring me . . .' (p. 14)

It is a rigid style which defines its objects crudely and
conveys a sense of arrogant authorial centainty.[4]

Such a strongly marked style does not fit easily with
other tones, but it does blend quite well with Aldington's commentary voice, found in passages where,
following Lawrence, the author intervenes to give
lectures, usually on social ethics and behaviour. This
voice appears reasonable, if slightly impatient:

> It was the régime of Cant *before* the War which made
> the Cant *during* the War so damnably possible and easy.
> On our coming of age the Victorians generously handed
> us a charming little cheque for fifty guineas – fifty-one
> months of hell, and the results. Charming people, weren't
> they? Virtuous and far-sighted. But it wasn't their fault?
> They didn't make the War. It was Prussia, and Prussian
> militarism? Right you are, right ho! Who made Prussia a
> great power and subsidized Frederick the Second to do it,
> thereby snatching an empire from France? England.
> Who backed up Prussia against Austria, and Bismarck
> against Napoleon III? England. And whose Cant gover-
> ned England in the nineteenth century? But never mind
> this domestic squabble of mine – put it that I mean the
> 'Victorians' of all nations. (p. 222)

This is the voice of the clear-sighted man of common
sense, the man from the University of Life who will not
be taken in by Fashion, Experts, or Idealism. In a
passage like this the voice is making sense enough, the
rhetorical questions and slangy litotes mocking facile
chauvinism. But it is a voice of little suppleness, one
which is reasonable so long as you agree with its
reasoning, but which suggests little interest in genuine

debate or in the exploration, of ideas, emotions or personalities. It is, in the last resort, a closed voice, vehicle of attitudes and angers potentially as dangerous (because as fixed) as those it attacks.

But Aldington has also, especially in Part III, a flatter, more restrained reporter's style, as here:

> They slept that night in a large German dug-out, swarming with rats. Winterbourne in his sleep felt them jump on his chest and face.
>
> The drum-fire began again next morning. Again they lined a trench and advanced through smoke over torn wire and shell-tormented ground. Prisoners passed through. At night they struggled for hours, carrying down wounded men in stretchers through mud and clamour. Major Thorpe was mortally wounded and his runner killed; Hume and his runner were killed; Franklin was wounded; Pemberton was killed; Sergeant Perkins was killed: the stretcher-bearers were killed. Men seemed to drop away continually. (p. 326)

More is conveyed in the tiny detail about the rats than in much hectic writing about the horrors of war, while 'Men seemed to drop away continually' is a highly effective generalization growing from the listing immediately before it.

This sort of writing dominates the final section, in which the war itself is central. The focusing on the fighting and the men involved in it reduces the satirical element, while at the same time providing the concrete justification for it. In this section Aldington gets beyond the impatient battering anger of the bulk of his novel, and also beyond the rather lofty authorial voice, writing with a sympathetic feeling for detail and with uncharacteristic restraint. But when this section is linked with the rest of the book awkward questions of control and coherence arise.

[51]

However, before turning to such questions, there is yet another style to be noticed, that of Aldington's affirmations. At times these are held, in relation to the novel's dominant satiric texture, by intimations of irony, as below in a phrase like 'the stately homes of Camden Town', in the inverted commas of 'frightfully' and the capital letters of 'the grey monster Ennui of Sunday-in-London':

> They were calling each other 'George' and 'Elizabeth' before they reached the stately homes of Camden Town. By the time they passed Mornington Crescent they had admitted that they liked each other 'frightfully' and would see a great deal of each other. In their excitement they talked rather incoherently, jumping from one topic to another in their eagerness to say something of all that seemed to clamour for expression, recklessly wasting their emotional energy. Their laughter had the ring of pure happiness ... Their natures expanded in a sudden delicious efflorescence; great coloured plumes of flowers seemed to sway and nod above their heads. They were enclosed in a nimbler air, the clear oxygen of desire, so compact, so resistant in the grey monster Ennui of Sunday-in-London. (pp. 149–50)

Elsewhere Aldington seems to be trying to evoke a more unqualified sense of verities:

> These are the gods, the gods who must endure for ever, or as long as man endures, the gods whom the perverse, blood-lustful, torturing Oriental myths cannot kill. Poseidon, the sea-god, who rules his grey and white steeds ... Selene, the moon-goddess, who flies so swiftly through the breaking clouds of the departing storm ... Phoebus, who scorns these silvery-grey northern lands, but whose golden light is so welcome when it comes. Demeter, who ripens the wheat and plumps the juicy fruit ... And then the lesser humbler gods – must there

not be gods of sunrise and twilight, of bird-singing and
midnight silence ... tenuous Ariel demi-gods of the
trembling poplars and the many-coloured flowers ... ? In
ever-increasing numbers the motor-cars clattered and
hammered along the dusty roads; the devils of golf leaped
on the acres and made them desolate; sport and journal-
ism and gentility made barren men's lives. The gods
shrank away, hid shyly in forgotten nooks ... Where
were their worshippers? Where were their altars? Rattle
of the motors, black smoke of the railways ... One alone
saw the fleet limbs glancing through the tree-trunks, saw
the bright faun-eyes peering anxiously from behind the
bushes. Hamadryads, fauns, do not fly from me! I am not
one of 'them', one of the perverse life-torturers ... Stay
with me, stay with me!
   Then the blow fell. (pp. 100–1)

The isolated 'Then the blow fell' makes the point of this
passage clear. But it is possible to sympathize with what
Aldington is trying to express while feeling that his
sense of loss is rigidly sentimental, an impotent lament,
sterile in its limited understanding, trapped in its
mythology. Where good Dickens is needed we have bad
Forster.

   Aldington is at pains to define the impulse behind his
novel – it is an effort at 'atonement'. 'Somehow or other
we have to make these dead acceptable, we have to
atone for them, we have to appease them. How, I don't
quite know' (p. 35). We have to appease them because
they are the ultimate victims 'of the whole sickening
waste of the war' and have the right to their vengeance;
we have to atone for them, to find a way of making their
losses good; we have to 'make these dead acceptable' in
the sense of registering and honouring them adequately
– but 'how, I don't quite know'. Only if we discover how
can we find an antidote to that which is poisoning us:

[53]

That is why I am writing the life of George Winterbourne, a unit, one human body murdered, but to me a
symbol. It is an atonement, a desperate effort to wipe off
the blood-guiltiness. (p. 36)

But as Aldington seeks to 'wipe off the blood-guiltiness'
he also seeks to involve us all in the struggle: 'I know
what is poisoning me. I do not know what is poisoning
you, but you are poisoned. Perhaps you too must atone'
(p. 36). What, then, can Aldington do for George
Winterbourne?

The ghost of Hamlet's father called for revenge.
Hamlet, surveying his task and the world which gave
rise to it, is both implicated and satirically angry.
Winterbourne needs to be appeased and the task falls
to Aldington-as-author. One thing he can do is to be
violently angry, but the anger is partly because, like
Hamlet, he is himself implicated. Early in the novel we
have one of the many onslaughts on George's progenitors:

To me, who only saw them a few times, either in
company with George or as his executor, they seemed as
fantastic, as ridiculous, as prehistoric as the returning
émigrés seemed in Paris in 1815. Like the Bourbons, the
elder Winterbournes learned nothing from the war, and
forgot nothing. (p. 23)

The war, as we saw earlier, transformed many things,
but 'It is the tragedy of England that the war has
taught its Winterbournes nothing . . . while the young
have simply chucked up the job in despair.' There is the
involvement: 'we go on acquiescing, we go on without
even the guts to kick the grotesque Aunt Sallies of
England into the limbo they deserve' (p. 23).

[54]

So, in part, *Death of a Hero* is an effort 'to kick the grotesque Aunt Sallies', the phrase being an accurate account of Aldington's satirized characters. And while this effort to kick is going on, it is also working to exonerate Winterbourne; product of the book's first section, what chance has he got?

But the anger which drives this novel also leads to its weakness, not because of the anger itself but because it betrays Aldington into confusion. Aldington tends not to think much beyond the rage: he attacks cliché with cliché, finding it impossible to break through the anger into some substantial commitment. When in *Life for Life's Sake,* he remarks 'They say I am bitter. The trouble is that I am not bitter enough' (p. 73) the sentiment is understandable, but the bitterness often limits perception.

In *Death of a Hero* confusion begins with Aldington's reaction to culture, the direct sarcastic common sense which is the book's dominant voice being suspicious of culture but itself quite clearly located (and limited) in cultural terms. Aldington attacks the educational values of the public schools for their emphasis on 'manliness' and their fear of art. The attitude is best summed up in the short story 'Sacrifice Post', where Davison realizes that 'The trouble was that it was almost impossible for an ordinary uneducated Public School man to think coherently, let alone express his feelings' (*Roads to Glory*, Chatto and Windus, 1930, p. 177). George Winterbourne is saved from the worst damage of this system by his own obstinate sensibility and by lucky encounters with truly educated individuals. The educational world of the novel is very close to that of Evelyn Waugh's autobiography (*A Little Learning,* Chapman and Hall, 1964) and it deserves the stricture it receives in both places. Unfortunately,

Aldington is more conditioned by this world than he seems to realize. He himself was educated at Dover College.

I mean by this that Aldington cannot take art seriously, as is very clear if his treatment of it is compared with Nevinson's account of his life in art at this period (*Paint and Prejudice,* Methuen, 1937). When Aldington tells us that George felt 'It was so much more fun to paint things than even to read what Keats and Shakespeare thought about them', he is obviously rendering George's youthful naïveties of response, as he again is when he tells how, on a visit to the Louvre, George 'simply leaped at the Italians and became very Pre-Raphaelite and adored the Primitives' (pp. 77–8). But the novel's response never gets much beyond this level.

Certainly Aldington attacks the philistines:

> The great English middle-class mass, that dreadful squat pillar of the nation, will only tolerate art and literature that are fifty years out of date, eviscerated, detesticulated, bowdlerized, humbuggered, slip-slopped, subject to their anglicized Jehovah . . . (p. 60)

Such people represent 'that unbroken rampart of Philistia against which Byron broke himself in vain, and which even the wings of Ariel were inadequate to surmount' (p. 60). In reacting against this Aldington abandons the bluff commonsense norm of his book in favour of that sentimental aestheticism which often betrays bluff commonsense. Something more robust than phrases about 'the wings of Ariel' would be needed before art could genuinely hope to infect life.

Two things characteristically happen when Aldington talks about art: he gets allusive and he gets snobbish. Both, I think, suggest that he has little sense of art as anything more than a Huysmans-like world of sensation for the leisured classes. This is even true in an essay like 'Artifex', in which Aldington mounts a formal defence of art as superior to science, business and theology. He defines art as 'servant of the life impulse, maker of myths, music and images' and, having personified it, goes on 'As we peer back through various epochs we see him dilate and diminish, like Milton's devil or Alice in Wonderland' (*Artifex*, Chatto and Windus, 1935, p. 11). There is the same distancing, the same belittling of art and life, when we are told in the story 'Now Lies She There' that with Constance 'The grave festival of the Muses became ... a Mad Hatter's tea-party' (*Soft Answers*, Chatto and Windus, 1932, p. 69). If art is indeed to be 'servant of the life impulse' it has to operate beyond the precious world of Ariel's wings and grave festivals of the Muses – but Aldington seems unable to realize this, most markedly at the end of this story, in which, having written quite impressively about wasted lives, he has his narrator retreat within this art-protected world of allusion:

> Morton interrupted my silence:
> 'Well? What do you think about it all?'
> 'I think', I said, rising to fill my glass, and lifting it, 'I think we owe a cock to Aesculapius.' (p. 122)

Indeed. And the snobbish triviality of so much of Aldington's thinking about art comes over very clearly in *Life for Life's Sake* when he talks of the impact of the Russian Ballet: 'there was already an intrusion of French influence which was regrettable. But it still remained the only completely satisfying artistic spectacle of my lifetime.' He then goes on to talk of the collapse of the ballet 'when London cockneys added "ov", "ski", and "evna" to their names, and produced a lamentable and lifeless parody of that once imperial art' (p. 207). What is wrong here is not the suggestion of the decline of the ballet but the sense that with the 'cockneys' there could be nothing but decline and the impression given that their adopting of Russian name-endings somehow caused it. Aldington, aware of public school philistinism, is himself a cultural snob, and the view of art he espouses dies from lack of oxygen.

This triviality of response underlies passages like that on the gods quoted earlier, and it weakens the impact of Aldington's attacks on the philistines, with the ultimate effect of creating uncertainty about the author's attitude to his protagonist. It is clear that Aldington is antagonistic to the commercialism he sees in the cultural world of London, a world in which George Winterbourne shows both integrity and inno-cence. But Aldington often seems unsure whether George is to be patronized or identified with. Here, for example, are George and Elizabeth, young in their young loves, before the coming of war:

> They walked on the grass through the long elm naves.
> 'How blue the sky is!' said Elizabeth, throwing back her head and breathing the soft air.
> 'Yes, and look how the elms make long Gothic arches!'
> 'Yes, and do look at the young leaves, so shrill, so virginal a green!'
> 'Yes, and the chestnut blossom will be out soon!'
> 'Yes, and the young grass is – Oh, Elizabeth look, look! The deer! There's two young ones.'
> 'Where? Where are they? I can't see them. I *want* to see them!' (p. 157)

It is hard to read such stuff and not to feel that the lovers are being gently mocked, and we may feel that, since this is formally a passage of reflection by a writer who has survived, the undercutting indicates how the war has touched everything, so that the love of George and Elizabeth is not invalidated, but seen, in the context of wider experience, as pathetically fragile and inefficacious – 'Peace be to you, O lovers, peace unto Juliet's grave!' (p. 156).

The reference to *Romeo and Juliet* may be important. Aldington's anger about the war involves him in almost total contempt for the generations which shaped the war, and he seems to have understood that his attacks on the hypocrisy and evil of George's progenitors have implications for George himself. Clearly we are meant to sympathize with George as victim of his upbringing, but at the same time that upbringing itself reduced the chances of George's being able to understand fully what he is, let alone attaining the freedom to achieve anything. So the retrospective picture of him in the park with Elizabeth is marked by the pathos of the doomed, but also with the superiority of the survivor over the victim.

Having seen the war through and – more important – having seen also the betrayal of the combatant in the post-war years, the author has the wisdom of almost total disillusionment, a wisdom not possible for George, whose death precludes the premature knowingness of the twenty-five-year-old veterans who crowd Aldington's books. And it is perhaps inevitable that the youthful idealism and optimism of George Winterbourne can only be seen, as Aldington looks back, with patronizing affection:

George was pretty much affected by this Social Reform bunk. He was always looking at things 'from the point of view of the Country', and far more frequently from 'the

[59]

> point of view of humanity'. This may have been a result
> of his Public School, kicked-backside-of-the-Empire
> training. (p. 162)

Distanced by disillusionment, Aldington finds it hard to
respond positively to anything, even to his own hero-
victim.

But this is not wholly true, for Aldington's cynicism
stops short of denying that, in the trenches, men were
capable of expressing their finest qualities. Early in the
novel he is emphatic about this: 'Friendships between
soldiers during the war were a real and beautiful and
unique relationship . . . It was just a human relation, a
comradeship, an undemonstrative exchange of sympathies between ordinary men racked by extremity
under a great common strain in a great common
danger' (pp. 30–1). This feeling for such comradeship
later leads Aldington to mitigate his reflex satire of the
officer Evans (p. 248 ff.) and it lies behind the bitter
anti-feminism which develops in the novel as the war
gains hold. In 'Sacrifice Post' Davison tries to reflect
upon such comradeship:

> Distinguish between true and false comradeship. Men
> instinctively have a sense of loyalty to each other, which
> is the basis of all human society. This is wilfully
> perverted by governments – instruments of the ambi-
> tious and destructive . . . (*Roads to Glory*, p. 175)

And in *Death of a Hero* Winterbourne looks at his
comrades: 'These men were men. There was something
intensely masculine about them, something very pure
and immensely friendly and stimulating . . . They
looked barbaric, but not brutal; determined, but not
cruel. Under their grotesque wrappings their bodies
looked lean and hard and tireless. They were Men'
(p. 253). Combining a high valuing of friendship with

[60]

this hardening-into-manliness theme might have led Aldington to find a way out of pessimism along Lawrentian lines, but he draws back from any such commitment. The sense of post-war disillusionment only allows appreciation of isolated decency in the war itself: there is no possibility of anything being built post-war which is either decent or a creation of the war. For Aldington is clear that the 'real and beautiful and unique relationship' has 'now entirely vanished, at least from Western Europe'. And the post-war moral climate is such that even this relationship has to be defended:

> Let me at once disabuse the eager-eyed Sodomites among my readers by stating emphatically once and for all that there was nothing sodomitical in these friendships. (pp. 30–1)

This is inherently unlikely, but the point now is that the war is seen as having encouraged friendship, out of which good might have come. But a mixture of the exhaustion which war induced in participants and the inability of non-combatants to learn what the war had been, meant that such comradeship was misunderstood, had therefore no chance of expanding into the post-war world, and has hence 'now utterly vanished'. Even that positive has been transformed.

If it is correct that the First World War involved transformation across the spectrum of European experience it is scarcely surprising that an intelligent and sensitive man like Aldington could do no more – even a decade after the war's end – than make negative sense of it. Certainly we should not be impatient about the cynical response of a man who was himself so burnt by his experiences. But (at the risk of seeming unwarrantably superior) it has to be said that to read Aldington now is to feel that his negative response rises from his limited sensibility. Like characters in Christopher Isherwood's *The Memorial* (Hogarth Press, 1932), it seems that Aldington was disabled by the war because his pre-war experience was too narrow for stability and not complacent enough for imperviousness. To say this of Aldington is not to isolate him, for few escaped unharmed, but it does mean that, post-war, he can find escape only in the fantasies of the final part of *All Men Are Enemies* (Chatto and Windus, 1933), with its spurious and sentimental mating of an Englishman who is a victim of war and an Austrian who is victim of her sex and nationality.

The perennial danger of satiric voices is that, depending – as they do – on simplification, they can become unperceptively distorting. Aldington's satiric voice needs brutality to drive home the onslaught on sexual and domestic ignorance before the war, these being seen as feeding the complacent bigotry which helped to make the war possible. But precisely the refusal to take account of shades, which is the strength of Aldington's best satire, works against him on other occasions. He talks, for instance, of social reformers, who perhaps proliferated, he speculates, 'due to the political idealism of Ruskin and Morris, aided by the infinitely more sensible work of the Fabians': 'Everybody was the architect of a New Jerusalem, and a rummy assortment of plans they provided. This passion has now reached the disinterested and noble-minded trade unionist and to some extent even the agricultural labourer' (p. 162). The voice seems confident, even cocky – and it hoists itself, being the voice of those who know about things without necessarily knowing things. There is no sign of real understanding of Ruskin or Morris; no demonstration of why the work of the

[62]

Fabians should be seen as 'infinitely more sensible'; a telling and betraying juxtaposition of 'idealism' with 'sensible'; the easy dismissiveness of 'a rummy assortment of plans' (can distinctions not be made among designs of New Jerusalems?); ambiguity of tone with the 'disinterested and noble-minded trade unionist'; and faint echoes of paternalism in the reference to agricultural labourers. *Death of a Hero* never engages seriously with the issues touched on by the passage just quoted, and Aldington's confidence of tone here, being unjustified, considerably weakens his novel.

When unjustified, such confidence does both negative and positive damage. The former arises because the manner is not fundamentally different from that of the philistines attacked. Is it any more culpable to refuse to understand the need for birth control and the fallacy of patriotism than to refuse to understand the thought and aims of William Morris or the social impulses which created trade unionism? Paradoxically, although Aldington cares passionately about what war did to people like Winterbourne, he seems unwilling to think seriously about those who had been working to change just the type of society which Aldington himself regards as responsible for the war. Here, I think, the pose of amateurism which was mentioned earlier really tells: Aldington is too much of a gentleman to be caught thinking hard about politics and ideas with a social context.

This leads to the positive harm caused by Aldington's rigid tone. He writes about the decades before 1914 and, less directly, about the immediate post-war years, as well as about the war itself; and he does so, to his credit, in an attempt to get a fix on the war instead of treating it in isolation. But his analysis, despite the overt hostility to Establishment values, is conducted with little awareness of significant alternatives to those values. Socialism – by which I mean here the work and writings of Marx and Engels, Lenin and Trotsky; even the rise of the Labour Party in Britain – is scarcely alluded to in *Death of a Hero*. It may be fair to say that the ignorance shown is an accurate reflection of the ignorance of most middle-class people in Britain in the war period, but Aldington is writing at the end of the twenties, and, since he is crying out against ignorance, cannot himself be excused for it. More importantly, this lack of knowledge and understanding cuts at the impact of the disillusionment basic to his novel. It can be argued that such disillusionment *accounts* for the tone of the passage on New Jerusalems, but there is no record of an attempt to understand – and thus no record of an effort against disillusionment. Here, perhaps, is the final sadness of Aldington: that the depression induced by the war prevents him even making the effort to understand those who tried to make war impossible or unrepeatable. Henri Barbusse's final vision of socialist brotherhood looks sadly dated in the light of Stalinist purges and of the violations of Hungary, Czechoslovakia and Poland; even in the light of contemporary Britain's betrayal of its welfare state. But Barbusse was able (and his sense of the filth of war was even more acute than Aldington's) to expand his responsiveness to that comradeship, of which Aldington writes, into a vision of a world which might live by the values of comradeship. His vision is still intensely moving, with the capacity to shake and lift the reader beyond cynicism and disappointment into renewed effort. Aldington's cynicism, however understandable and however 'justified' by events, can never be more than a shield forged out of pain. The slight gains we make in humanity – the times we refrain from war; the erratic fostering of the poor, sick and underprivileged – are only made from a refusal to be always cynical. Perhaps the best way of atoning for George Winterbourne lies in refusing to accept that Aldington must be right, for if he is we are all essentially dead.

III

The Return of the Soldier

Richard Aldington's Winterbourne never returned home. Sickened and saddened by the war, in both its front and home manifestations, he exposed himself to German fire in a kind of suicide, while Henry Williamson's Bullock returned home injured and was soon embittered by what he found there.

Many had seen the war as fought to save civilization from the Hun, or as being the war to end wars, the final act of humanity's folly and precursor to eternal peace. Those who fought were encouraged to see themselves as voluntary sacrifices to ensure a better world for their country, their families and themselves, yet, for many who survived, the post-war reality was bitter: unemployment, the reassertion of social divisions, the rapid fading of whatever heroic status they may have held. Robert Wohl has studied some of the effects of the war upon survivors in the post-war years (*The Generation of 1914*, Weidenfeld and Nicolson, 1980), but it is worth adding that the sense of exhaustion which is so marked a feature of the closing stages of the war continues in post-war years and is reflected, for instance, in the brittle sophistication of Aldous Huxley's *Crome Yellow* (1921) and in the disillusionment of Eliot's *The Waste Land* (1922).

In a sense there were three ways in which a combatant might finally return from the war. If he was killed his body would not normally return, but there was the return of his effects and the letter of condolence. He might return as a casualty to be invalided out of the forces, or fit only for home duty. He might return, technically still fully fit, after the Armistice. There were many returns, of course, and in this chapter I want to look at four treatments in fiction of the figure of the returning soldier, one of these a return which is metaphysical rather than literal.

Gilbert Frankau's *Peter Jackson, Cigar Merchant* ends in London with the Armistice, with glasses being clinked 'in token of civilisation's triumph over the Beast' (p. 399), but Peter himself and Francis Gordon, cousin to his wife Pat, had been invalided well before the end, both suffering mentally as well as physically, and the novel's final section is an account of how Frankau's chief characters are made fit for peace.

Francis Gordon had been shaped by his devotion to literature, but when Pat meets him after he has been invalided he is a broken man:

> She remembered him a smooth-faced boy, she saw him now a middle-aged man. His hair had grayed at the temples; his eyes had lost their laughter . . . he no longer held himself upright, his shoulders drooped as though he carried a burden on them. (p. 322)

To Patricia the question is 'would Francis ever be well again; well in mentality; able to reconstruct his life?'. Her instinct says no, and 'her fantasy pictured him a stricken beast, crawling away to die in solitude' (p. 323). One thinks of Aldington's devastated figures and of Graves on the stamina of neurasthenia (*Goodbye to All That,* p. 143 ff.).

Patricia, making her 'last bid for Peter's love', has found and occupied a country cottage, 'the little house she, Patricia, would make "home" for her man against his return from the wars' (p. 320). But Peter returns wounded in one arm and contracts bronchial pneumonia, almost dying of the latter. As he recovers in body, however, 'he grew aware of new dangers'. These take the form of fears – in sleep and daylight, of the present and the future, of time, pain and poverty, of returning to the front, of not returning, of consumption:

> Peter did not realize that these fears were among the commonest symptoms of neurasthenia. Peter knew nothing about neurasthenia . . . His fears shamed him; and so he hid them away. (p. 328)

Like Francis, Peter is a war casualty, and Patricia's fantasy applies as much to him as to her cousin. Yet both men are rendered fit enough to celebrate the Armistice, the 'triumph over the Beast'. How?

The sort of shock experienced by Peter and Francis is not the kind which can be fully anticipated and catered for. The phenomenon which was the Great War tested men in new ways, or at least more extremely than anything in the previous history of war. Peter's fears represent the degree of breakdown which Sassoon caught so well in his poem 'Repression of War Experience', and there is little protection against such worms in the psyche. Possibly the strain was greater for the more privileged, lacking the endurance of those partly inured to hardship by pre-war conditions, but neurasthenia was no respecter (not even an ironic one) of class or rank.

Nevertheless, given the damage to Peter and Francis, their social status helps to explain their recoveries. Being officer-class they are individuals worthy of respect

and attention. More specifically, Patricia's class means
that she will not be put off by people like the matron of
Peter's hospital ('a forbidding woman of uncertain age',
p. 324) or like the registrar of the same hospital ('a
pompous but kindly individual', p. 324). She has the
class-confidence to command attention and deference,
but she also has the fictional good fortune to be the
daughter of a prominent neuro-surgeon. When the
hospital comes to know this the advantages are clear:

> The hospital staff, knowing her Heron Baynet's daugh-
> ter, made full amends: Matron grew kindly; neglectful
> sister was unremitting in service . . . (p. 327)

Heron Baynet recognizes what is wrong with Peter and
Francis: they and Patricia have the advantage of his
time and advice. But this opportune help is not the key
to the recoveries of these returned soldiers, though it
facilitates the unlocking of their neuroses. The key is
love.

In the case of Francis this works largely at the level
of the plot's assertions. Francis's love for the American
Beatrice Cochrane is interrupted at its inception by the
war, and Francis feels it wrong to remind her of his
feelings since he is damaged by the war. Patricia,
however, writes to Beatrice, who, in the manner of
romance, comes to England and saves Francis from
despair:

> His eyes . . . saw a shadow glide across the room
> towards him . . .
> 'Beatrice,' he stammered, 'Beatrice!'
> Words went from them. They stood speechless. Their
> hands met in the twilight. Lips faltered to lips. Then she
> was in his arms, and God grew real at last. (p. 372)

[69]

Patricia is instrumental in the salvation of Francis, but her major task is to save her husband. She first does this by suspecting his pneumonia, alerting the doctor at the hospital to this, and calling in her father, but her real triumph is psychological. Baynet urges Patricia to make Peter talk:

> Make him drunk if you like – get drunk yourself – make love to him as if you were his mistress: but for God's sake, make him talk. (p. 336)

Patricia comes gradually to see that 'in clean desire, love sanctifying, could be no shame' (p. 340); acts accordingly; saves Peter.

So love provides salvation, God again grows real, and Frankau assimilates his returned soldiers into the traditional comic harmony of the dance:

> Everybody was dancing. The flags were dancing. Men and women were dancing. Soldiers were dancing ... lame soldiers and legless soldiers and armless soldiers – ill soldiers and well soldiers. Sailors were dancing ... The very houses were dancing ... Their own car was dancing ... the blood was dancing in their veins, dancing and dancing ... (p. 399)

Civilization has triumphed over the Beast, Patricia's marriage has been saved, the Old Country and the New are united in Francis and Beatrice, the ecstasy of Armistice Day overrides the agonies and fears: the dance, it seems, will go on and on ...

It is hardly necessary to say that this is rubbish. Frankau has substituted slickness of plot for seriousness of purpose, sentimentality for analysis, fantasy for history. All he renders, despite seeming to be aware of the vileness of war, is a complacent conservatism. His officer soldiers return to sexy rewards, to 'the dancing wine of Francis' forethought from gold-foiled bottle neck' (p. 399) and to his 'inarticulate "E–ton! Well rowed, E–ton" ' (p. 398). 'Our men' are toasted, 'our splendid, splendid men!', but it is, at the level of Frankau's novel, the sentimentality of champagne. The interesting war has been a race in which Eton men have rowed. Nothing changes, nothing is learnt; yet my edition, of 1920, claims to be the twentieth, representing 67,000 copies.

Frankau's 'men' are never more than shadows, for although Frankau has some glib awareness of class he knows almost nothing about society at large. The essence of his England is middle-class metropolitan and even there everything is stereotyped, incapable of significant change. By contrast Arnold Bennett shows a real sense of society as a complex, animate reality, and his awareness of the intricacy of social organisms, together with his feeling for the interaction of personality, environment and tradition, makes him at his best a genuine social novelist. Being such a novelist, Bennett could hardly ignore the Great War, and in *Lord Raingo* (1926) his consideration includes the figure of Geoffrey, Raingo's son, and specifically his return from the war.

As its title indicates, Bennett's novel is primarily a presentation of the consciousness of the eponymous Sam Raingo, Geoffrey being part of his consciousness. To a large extent, then, we are not so much asked to consider Geoffrey and his return as to respond to Sam's sense of his son and that return. Raingo is a self-conscious public figure, but since he not only has a private life but an awareness of it, some conscience about what he says and does, and also a marked ironic awareness of the disparity between his origins and his present social and political standing, Geoffrey is important to him not only as his son (and therefore his future) but as his representative in a war he is too old to fight in, but which he influences through his ministerial function.

Raingo is acutely aware of the war, and this goes well beyond mere administrative consciousness to include an imaginative grasp of the pervasiveness of the war at home. So, for instance, when Raingo is being introduced to the House of Lords, 'He felt like a recruit, a conscript', and he reflects that 'this, too, is part of the war':

> His uneasy mind ranged over the immeasurable panorama of the war: the ministerial departments contending with one another ... the clangour of the factories, the bland disdain of imprisoned conscientious objectors, the private agonies of the parents of young conscripts ... all the blood and mud and roar and shrieking of the battlefields, and ... the veiled lands where the enemy planned more destruction ... and his son Geoffrey, who had had the guts to escape from those lands and was now – somewhere. (Cassell, 1926, p. 168)

Geoffrey here has a context and is significant of that context, as is again the case a few pages later, when Raingo is in the room in which his wife lies dead:

> On the bed lay the symbol and summing up of all the war-grief and fatigue of the world. The universe was old and spent. The war continued desperately – but mechanically, of its own inertia of desperation. Where was Geoffrey? (p. 179)

Sam Raingo is proud enough and administrator enough not to let his imagination and private consciousness overcome his sense of service and function, but Bennett's awareness of both elements is what makes Raingo interesting. When, then, the funeral procession on the way to bury Raingo's wife stops

[72]

suddenly, Sam is 'impatient at this flaw in the perfection of the arrangements'. The flaw is the returned Geoffrey and 'Sam could not speak for a second, so shocked and frightened was he by the intensity of his own emotion'. The administrative and the personal intersect, and Raingo, who depends so much on 'the perfection of the arrangements', now has to bear not only the stress of his wife's death, but the return of his son from the front, not as a mature figure to support him but as a neurotic who 'began to pull nervously at the front of his khaki collar, twitching his neck again and again to the right' (pp. 182–3).

In Frankau's novel there was the neuro-surgeon to explain damaged minds and offer healing advice. But Lord Raingo is a central character who, like Baynet, is in a position of power, the difference being that Raingo gets trapped, despite his intelligence, in his own propaganda. Geoffrey does not correspond to the image that his father has been concerned to propagate:

[Sam] had thought that young soldiers were men who fought passionately for country, took orders, obeyed orders, and enjoyed themselves wildly when they could – and didn't argue nor reflect. Now he stood like a tongue-tied criminal at the judgment-seat of his fierce and dangerous son – yesterday a boy, to-day an old, damaged, disillusioned man. (pp. 185–6)

The fierceness, disillusionment and non-communication have to be borne because Sam Raingo is not hollow or mechanical, but the transformation of Geoffrey is appalling because it is a product of an activity which Sam lives to justify in public. So when, a few pages later, Geoffrey, crying, leaves his father, Raingo reflects 'Politics! Titles! Propaganda! What odious,

[73]

contemptible tinsel and mockery. Here was the war itself, tragedy, utterly distracted fatherhood.' (p. 190)

But Geoffrey's return comes less than half-way through Bennett's novel and his neurasthenia is not Bennett's main concern. The chief interest is in Raingo himself, in the relationships between private and public beings and between success and futility, and it is to Bennett's credit that he presents Raingo's vanity and pride – 'He had taught Andy and the War Cabinet and the famous fighting services a lesson. He longed for more press-cuttings. His appetite for press-cuttings was gluttonous' (p. 277) – without making him a ludicrous figure. There is absurdity in the declining Raingo's concern with his public standing, but there is also the rendering of integrity and achievement. Therefore, when Bennett, near the end, writes that 'All the life of the house was gathered round the toxin-ridden organism on the Empire bed' (p. 408) there is a fine balance of pathos: Raingo *is* a 'toxin-ridden organism', but he has tried to understand himself and to serve his world.

As Raingo declines we are shown Geoffrey as not simply a 'damaged, disillusioned man'. Geoffrey begins to find a way back when he takes over the redecoration of the family house, and he becomes a strength for his father to draw on. Moreover, he falls in love with Gwen, sister of Sam's mistress, Delphine. By the end of the book Geoffrey and Gwen have emerged as strong people in their own right and, therefore, a source of hope for the future. But there is no simple sense that Geoffrey has recovered from the war. He can cope with home, even succeed there, but he remains a detached, commanding figure, with an independence, almost a wisdom, which cannot be assimilated to the complacent conservatism of a Frankau. Bennett's returned soldier

[74]

is not a casualty of the Aldington type, but he *has* been damaged and made disillusioned, and he operates at home by lessons learnt at the front. In that sense he is kin to Romains' marauders, Lawrence's Diggers and the author-figure of Jünger's *Storm of Steel* (Jules Romains, *Verdun*, 1938; D. H. Lawrence, *Kangaroo*, 1932; Ernst Jünger, *Im Stahlgewittern*, 1920). Like these, he operates on his own terms and, if society is to reintegrate him, it must change.

Since Bennett is not primarily concerned with the war at the front it is perhaps not surprising that there is no final placing of Geoffrey. Yet, focused upon the life and slow passing of Sam Raingo, in a way which incorporates Geoffrey, Bennett's novel is concerned with the passing of a generation which, while being too old to fight in the war, nevertheless was the generation which made it and controlled it (in so far as any people did). Raingo's generation not only made Geoffrey's but also remade or unmade its representatives in the experience of the war, and Bennett seems to have sensed that this remaking necessitated change. The soldier returns altered, if not destroyed; and Geoffrey seems to mark Bennett's awareness that the returnee cannot be changed back in the way Frankau would wish. Bennett is no prophet: the good social novelist is, rather, responsive to change in the contemporary social organism. The rise of such men as Chamberlain and Lloyd George, together with the broader significance of the establishment of the Labour Party, indicated deep social change in Britain, and Bennett's Raingo, Clyth and Jenkin show his awareness of this. But the Great War encouraged and accelerated various kinds of radicalism, and Bennett's Geoffrey – never a central character – shows that Bennett sensed as much, which saved him from Frankau's flaccid sentimentality.

The meeting between Sam and Geoffrey Raingo on the latter's return from France has its analogy in that between Wells's Britling and the young Teddy in *Mr Britling Sees It Through*. Teddy's return plays a part in the re-education of Britling and is presented as one element in the participation of four young men in the war. Britling's son Hugh, whose letters provide the novel's main statements about direct participation in the war, is killed before Teddy's return. His death is matched by that of the young German, Heinrich, a guest at Matching's Easy at the outset of war. The fourth young man is another visitor, the American Direck, who, having argued the case for American non-intervention, finally joins the Canadian forces.

It is Britling's 'seeing it through' which we are asked to concentrate upon, but he is *paterfamilias* at Matching's Easy and the novel examines the war's impact not only upon Britling himself but upon the whole circle of the house; house and circle being seen as a microcosm of traditional (pastoral) England.[1] The informal games of hockey which are a feature of social life at Matching's Easy provide a symbol of that life, involving visitors as well as guests and residents, and merging the generations in corporate activity. Hugh sees his first experience of combat as being 'as exciting as one of those bitter fights we used to have round the hockey-goal' (p. 221). He also says 'I'd seen death and killing, and it was all just hockey' (p. 223). Wells is obviously using the analogy between war and sport to suggest the innocence of the ninteen-year-old Hugh, and, beyond this, of the context from which he comes. Further, the innocent game of life at Matching's Easy is interrupted by the sombre 'game' of the Great War, and Teddy's return is the literal incursion of the latter into the former.

[76]

The news that Teddy is wounded and missing is given to the reader almost immediately after Hugh's remarks just quoted, 'while figs were still ripening on Mr Britling's big tree', casting an obvious ironic shadow on both of these. So long as the news remains merely of Teddy as 'wounded and missing' he exists in a state between life and death in the minds of his family, and particularly in the mind of his wife, Letty. As Hugh says, 'Missing's a queer thing. It isn't tragic – or pitiful. Or partly reassuring like "prisoner". It just sends one speculating and speculating' (p. 221). The tension of the situation tells particularly on Letty, representative of Matching's Easy. It corrodes and darkens her responses:

> . . . if people like Teddy are to be killed, then all our ideas that life is meant for honesty and sweetness and happiness are wrong, and this world is just a place of devils; just a dirty cruel hell. (p. 235)

From bitterness come plans for revenge – 'I shall get just as close to the particular Germans who made this war as I can, and I shall kill them and theirs . . .' (p. 236). Letty's sister, Cissie, sees 'All this tense scheming of revenge' as 'the imaginative play with which Letty warded off the black alternative to her hope; it was not strength, it was weakness' (p. 238). Under this sustained pressure Letty, civilized child of Matching's Easy, turns from the liberal tolerance of the tradition to the hard-edged, war-perpetuating revenger – from hockey pitch to the Somme.

A change comes, however, when Letty, now believing Teddy to be dead, talks, significantly in the open countryside, with Britling, who is grieving for Hugh. Typically, Britling seeks to draw general conclusions, a philosophy, from what has happened:

[77]

The world is weary of this bloodshed, weary of all this weeping, of this wasting of substance, and this killing of sons and lovers ... I will write of nothing else, I will think of nothing else now but of safety and order. (p. 246)

Letty is unreceptive at this point: '[The world] is just a place of cruel things. It is all set with knives. It is full of diseases and accidents. As for God – either there is no God or he is an idiot. He is a slobbering idiot' (p. 246). But slowly Britling gets through to her with his sense of a God 'who struggles, who was in Hugh and Teddy, clear and plain, and how he must become the ruler of the world' (p. 248). So, learning from this 'changed and simplified man' (p. 248), Letty experiences a reaction:

Letty who had gone out with her head full of murder and revenge, came back through the sunset thinking of pity, of the thousand kindnesses and tendernesses of Teddy that were after all, perhaps, only an intimation of the limitless kindnesses and tendernesses of God ... (p. 249)

This changed perception 'earns' Letty a reprieve, which comes on her return home, where she sees 'a stranger, a foreigner' who is the wounded Teddy – 'If she did not get to him speedily the world would burst' (p. 250).

As Letty regains 'poor broken Teddy' (p. 252), Cissie loses Direck – 'I suppose I must let you go ... Oh! I'd hate you not to go ...' (p. 252) – and Mr Britling is left with his grief for Hugh and with whatever he can make of it. From his contemplation of his loss and of the parallel death of Heinrich comes the full development of the deism expressed to Letty:

... life falls into place only with God. Only with God. God, who fights through men against Blind Force and Night and Non-Existence; who is the end, who is the meaning ...

Our sons ... have shown us God ... (p. 269)

[78]

Wells's novel ends with 'Wave after wave of warmth and light ... sweeping before the sunrise across the world of Matching's Easy'. *Mr Britling* is finally a visionary novel, Wells using his sense of contemporary actuality as basis for a vision of the future (to be acted out, as it happened, in the idealism of the League of Nations, which became a parody of its own ideals). The return of Teddy is part of the pattern which makes up this vision. At the level of the mundane Hugh and Heinrich are dead, Direck is at risk, and Teddy is 'poor broken Teddy', his missing arm the mark of the damage of war. Wells does not ignore the pain and corrosion, but we are finally to see all this as falling into place 'with God', and to accept that the loss of Hugh and Heinrich, with the breaking of Teddy, 'have shown us God'. *Mr Britling* was published in 1916: the intervening years make it hard to respond to this sublimation other than ironically. Teddy's return to Letty seems Wells's gift to her – the reward for her reaction into pity – but Wells was badly wrong about what was to follow, for there has been little sign of 'Wave after wave of warmth and light'. In that sense Teddy's return is futile: 'It is all set with knives.'

Frederic Manning's hero, Bourne, does not literally return from the front at all, but dies fighting there. Like millions of other soldiers Bourne travels to the war and is tested by it, but Bourne's testing involves a return, under the pressures of war, to the centre of his being, where, after a metaphysical journey, he finds peace. In this sense *The Middle Parts of Fortune* contrasts strongly with Bensted's *Retreat*: the war breaks the Anglican padre, Warne, whereas Manning's Bourne dies in philosophical peace.

Novels which focus upon trench experience in the Great War are frequently and understandably angry in tone, and they tend to include, in greater or less detail, an effort to provide a context for the war, to set it in a social and/or economic environment. In both ways novels like Aldington's *Death of a Hero* and Wilfrid Ewart's *Way of Revelation* (Putman, 1921) are typical. Manning's novel is unusual both for its patient tone and because, among 'serious' war novels, it is curiously devoid of context. There is no effort to provide an account of how its hero, Bourne, comes to be the sort of man he is, and Manning is not (at least explicitly) concerned with wider issues of 'how', 'why' and 'what now', such as preoccupy Aldington. Manning is, in fact, primarily interested in the First World War as autonomous phenomenon. His novel has implications, of course, but he does not seek to provide an explicit context: for him the war is organic and morally almost neutral, and although he renders the filth, pettiness, and horror he also sees the war as providing the chance for Man to show his finest qualities and as encouraging a philosophical ripeness which, as in stoicism, can give the individual serenity in face of whatever the gods may serve up. Such an attitude to the war can reasonably be called epic: in his introduction to the 1977 edition Michael Howard links *The Middle Parts of Fortune* with Aeschylus, while Ernest Hemingway once called it 'the noblest book of men in war'.

References to Aeschylus and stoicism, in relation to a novel about a modern war, may make that novel sound self-consciously literary, or as if concerned with the kind of individual heroic actions which win Victoria Crosses. But Manning has, at his best, a fine sense of textural detail which tests values even as it embodies them, and his novel is directly concerned with 'the anonymous ranks'. But this latter concern emerges neither as primarily social nor as a propagandist desire

[80]

that the rankers should receive their due. It is, rather, a matter of where Manning locates the essence of the war experience; for 'the weight of the war falls on the ordinary soldier: ... what is called, in the British Army, the chain of responsibility, which means that all responsibility for the errors of their superior officers, is borne eventually by private soldiers in the ranks' (p. 166). Or there are Bourne's similar comments earlier:

> I may tell you that there are precious few mistakes made in the army that are not ultimately laid on the shoulders of the men. (p. 95)

This attitude is linked with the contrast between Staff and troops of the line:

> 'They don't know what we've got to go through, that's the truth of it,' said Weeper. 'They measure the distance, an' think a battle's no' but a sum you do wi' a pencil an' a bit o'paper.' (p. 154)

And this sense of 'us' extends to the feeling both of being special and of being misunderstood by those back home:

> 'Well, chaps,' said Glazier, 'maybe I'm right an' maybe I'm wrong ... only I've sometimes thought it would be a bloody good thing for us'ns, if the 'un did land a few troops in England. Show 'em what war's like. Madely an' I struck it lucky an' went 'ome on leave together, an' you never seed anything like it. Windy! Like a lot o' bloody kids they was, an' talkin' no more sense; 'pon me word, you'd be surprised at some o' the questions they'd ask, an' you couldn't answer sensible ...' (p. 152)

There is no doubt that, in moments like this, Manning is registering responses which were real in war experience, but he does not seem very interested in the social implications of the responses – they are

[81]

registered to be explored philosophically rather than sociologically. The key to Manning's individual treatment of common themes and attitudes lies in one of the novel's few directly religious moments, the encounter with the stone calvary discussed in chapter I. I suggested there that Manning does not make anything of the idea of Christ as humankind's light into the hereafter. Bourne's death is not a return to the bosom of Abraham, and Manning completely avoids the obscene religiosity of such productions as *The Child of Flanders* (*One Act Plays of Today,* ed. J. W. Marriott, Harrap, 1925). But he does propose that soldiers experienced suffering to a degree which identifies them with the crucified Christ. As crucifixion both tests and justifies Christ, so the war 'proves' the men Manning is concerned with.

Manning is as aware as Aldington of the awful shocks and pressures of war in the front line. The opening of his novel treats men suffering the consequences of bombardment, attack, and heavy losses; and the officer, Clinton, speaks to Bourne in terms Aldington would recognize:

> 'Come on,' he said, making for the steps, 'you and I are two of the lucky ones, Bourne; we've come through without a scratch; and if our luck holds we'll keep moving out of one bloody misery into another, until we break, see, until we break.' (p. 4)

Aldington's Winterbourne breaks, offers himself to German bullets as the only way of coping, and *Death of a Hero* is concerned to indict a society which creates such suicides. Manning's Bourne understands Clinton's 'angry soreness', but *The Middle Parts of Fortune* is not an Aldington novel and Bourne replies to Clinton:

'Don't talk so bloody wet... You'll never break.'
Manning's is a novel of not breaking.

The comments quoted earlier serve to isolate the
front line troops from Staff and non-combatants. The
former suffer the most, and that is their agony and, in
this novel, their privilege, since it allows them (indeed
forces them) to 'know Christ crucified'. They are
enabled to do this because the pressures on them create
a taut collectivism, which Manning pins down early in
his novel:

> Among themselves they were unselfish, even gentle;
> instinctively helping each other, for, having shared the
> same experience, there was a tacit understanding
> between them. They knew each other and their rival
> egoisms had already established among them a balance
> and discipline of their own. (p. 12)

What Manning is concerned with is something which is
not the product of the army's overt values – the
'balance and discipline' of which he writes are their
own, 'constituting the uniformity, quite distinct from
the effect of military discipline, which their own nature
had imposed on them' (p. 40). Nor is this anything to do
with thought, education or civilization: it is 'tacit', a
matter of instinct, for these men 'had lapsed a little
lower than savages, into the mere brute'. And it is not a
matter of losing self in a greater whole: rather it is
'rival egoisms' in equilibrium, for 'self-reliance lies at
the very heart of comradeship' (p. 149). Comradeship,
for Manning, is a paradox – 'the spiritual thing in them
which lived and seemed even to grow stronger, in the
midst of beastliness' (p. 141).

This 'spiritual thing', however, has little or nothing
to do with faith in the Christian sense. Manning may
use the image of Christ on the cross, but he makes

[83]

nothing of ideas of resurrection and the afterlife. What he apprehends and celebrates is seen in Stoic terms: the men can 'master' their 'vices and appetites' with 'rather a splendid indifference':

> These apparently rude and brutal natures comforted, encouraged, and reconciled each other to fate, with a tenderness and tact which was more moving than anything in life.

They said 'with a passionate conviction that it would be all right, though they had faith in nothing, but in themselves and in each other' (p. 205).

War has induced in these men a lapsing into a state 'a little lower than savages', but it is in this state that they find themselves and each other. Given this view it is not surprising that direct comments on the war are far from simple condemnation. Bourne, reflecting remarks made by Sergeant Tozer, considers that 'life was a hazard enveloped in mystery, and war quickened the sense of both in men', so that the soldier, like the saint, may write his 'tractate *de contemptu mundi*', differing from the saint 'only in the angle and spirit from which he surveyed the same bleak reality' (p. 76). If reality is bleak, war is only an extension of existing bleakness, an intensification perhaps, but not an aberration. And Bourne, feeling life 'a hazard enveloped in mystery', can respond to war as making men 'return' to fuller life, while to Aldington the Great War was an occasion only of physical and spiritual death.

Although, as suggested earlier, Manning seems to see war as a natural phenomenon, it does not follow that Man is not responsible for himself in war. Rather the reverse: it is in war most of all that Man is fully responsible. It is in this sense that Manning writes in his prefatory note that 'War is waged by men; not by beasts or by gods. It is a peculiarly human activity.' Being thus part of what human reality is, and since we are responsible for our reality, 'To call [war] a crime against mankind is to miss at least half its significance; it is also the punishment of a crime.' So it is possible for Bourne to think 'the war as a moral effort was magnificent' (p. 92). Manning does not pin down this idea of war as being 'as much punishment of a crime' as itself criminal in specific moral or political terms. He is more concerned with the experiential effect. War can produce the comradeship spoken of above, and it can induce such a 'feeling of certitude in a peace so profound, that all the turmoil of the earth was lost in it' (p. 208). What is particularly important here is that Bourne thinks of 'all the turmoil of the *earth*': war, again, is at one with human reality, and in it peace can be found which will embrace all experience: Bourne, through his encounter with war, returns to such knowledge.

Whether or not I am correct in feeling that Manning concentrated upon private soldiers because he felt that the 'mystery' of war was at its richest in them, or whether he had a more propagandist purpose, he had a technical problem to solve when he decided to concern himself with the common soldier. It would have been possible to write a novel about the men as seen by an officer, but such a novel, by definition, could scarcely be from within, and Manning needs inwardness. How then to achieve inwardness with plausibility, when few private soldiers had the education to articulate the outlook central to the novel? Manning's answer is to have as his hero a man from the formally educated classes who has decided to enlist as a ranker. Manning himself did just this, joining the Shropshire Light Infantry as a private in 1914, and refusing a commission. This autobiographical link means, of course, that some of the implications of Bourne's role may be accidental rather than planned. Manning may simply be writing from the viewpoint he happened to know best, rather than operating as a notionally fully self-conscious novelist, devising technical solutions to technical difficulties. But speculations are less important than results.

Bourne is picked out right at the start of the novel. The opening words close in from 'darkness', 'whole sky' and 'thunder' to the anonymous 'they', who 'return to their original line as best they could', and then to Bourne, 'who was beaten to the wide' and 'gradually dropped behind'. At this stage we can know nothing about him or his function, but he is to prove a formal focus of the novel, a figure of some complexity; and the separateness of Bourne, indicated in these opening lines, is important. Bourne 'had a text of Horace with Conington's translation in his pocket' (p. 56). Reflecting on Martlow and his domestic attitudes he feels 'great admiration for the impartial candour with which Martlow looked back on family life' (p. 114) – here the phrasing separates Bourne from Martlow himself. His speech uses the shapes of education: 'If they can do anything backwards in the army, they will, you know. It's the tradition of the service . . .' (p. 171). He can even sound slightly, if benevolently, patronizing to his fellows: 'Can't you take an ordinary telling-off without starting to grouse about it?' (p.49).

Such moments work to isolate Bourne, but it is significant that his isolation is not defined in specifically cultural terms. At one point he explains to Captain Malet why he is reluctant to go for a commission, telling him that when the adjutant had raised the same question at his enlistment 'I told him that I had absolutely no experience of men, not even the kind of experience that a public-school boy gets from being one of a larger community' (p. 90). Later he has a moment of awkwardness with Captain Marsden, 'for although the conventions which separated officers from men were relaxed to some extent on active service, between men of roughly the same class they tended to become more rigid' (p. 229). This is almost all the explicit information we are given – and it merely confirms Bourne's ambiguous position.

Yet Bourne is not some kind of spy, sent to observe the characteristics of the workers. He has decided to opt in, and – more important – operates as a link. This is an exact image, for a link is part of what it unites, even while it and those things are not the same. So Bourne, while remaining socially officer-class, is simultaneously also a private soldier, in more than rank. The tension is recognized by the novel, and indeed by Bourne himself: 'Bourne often found himself looking at his companions as it were from a remote distance' – but this is because 'he was merely wondering how far what he felt himself was similar or equivalent to what they felt'. He goes on to imagine 'that the other men were probably a little less reflective and less reasonable than he was himself', while he 'frankly envied them the wanton and violent instincts, which seemed to guide them . . . so successfully through this hazardous adventure'. The paragraph ends with a shift which is also a repetition:

> They had accepted him, and he mucked in with them quite satisfactorily. But there was a question which every man put to another at their first acquaintance: What did you do in civil life? (p. 39)

The recognition of the details of difference and the sense of a two-way process indicate a sensitivity to unlikeness which validates the sharing: it is equivalent, at the class level, to the paradox of self-reliance and comradeship.

Bourne never acquires a Christian name. The last thoughts about him come from Tozer after his death. Tozer looks at the dead body:

> . . . it wasn't a pleasant sight . . . Bourne was sitting: his head back, his face plastered with mud, and blood drying quickly about his mouth and chin, while the glazed eyes stared up at the moon. (p.247)

Tozer 'moved away, with a quiet acceptance of the fact. It was finished.' As Tozer moves away he thinks that Bourne 'was a queer chap . . . There was a bit of a mystery about him; but then, when you come to think of it, there's a bit of a mystery about all of us.' The novel ends a few lines later with the survivors listening to the German shelling, 'each man keeping his own secret'.

What this makes clear is that Bourne is central, in more than a formal sense, to Manning's novel. The fact that he is with the men but not wholly of them makes his death typical in a way which goes beyond class, while Tozer's echo of Christ's 'consummatum est' reminds us of the soldiers' identification earlier with the crucifixion, Bourne's body acting here as connective icon. Even Tozer's 'quiet acceptance' goes through Bourne, back to the serenity the latter had come to feel, and the juxtaposition of this with the physical foulness of the corpse holds the novel's paradoxical quality to the end.

We are, as mentioned earlier, told little of Bourne's background – in fact, we are told little of the background of any of the characters – and this leads to another paradox. It might seem that Manning withholds context because he wants Bourne to be representative in the manner of Williamson's Bullock. But Bourne is not truly representative of anything but himself – nor could he be.

In the first place Bourne is far from an Everyman. We may know little about his pre-war life but we come to know a good deal about him. Some of his characteristics – the volume of Horace, the benevolent patronage, the ability to admire Martlow – have been touched on earlier, and it can be added that he is an accomplished scrounger (quite capable of using class to circumvent deficiencies of rank), sardonic, even malicious. He is certainly not a type, and the same might be said for several other characters, notably Shem, Martlow, Weeper and Miller.

But the real reason why Bourne cannot be representative in Williamson's sense lies in Manning's outlook. To the extent that Bourne is a 'comrade' he represents comradeship, but to the extent that he is self-reliant and a mystery he stands only for himself. This is reflected in the fact that we know little of his history: he firmly *is*, but he doesn't analytically *mean*. And this is important in another sense. The war is such a phenomenon that what came before it has little meaning (an outlook quite unlike Aldington's) while what you are, as you seek to cope with the phenomenon, is everything.

As its subtitle ('Somme and Ancre, 1916') suggests, *The Middle Parts of Fortune* is so firmly a novel about the Great War that it is a novel about one small part of the war – not even really 'Somme and Ancre' but 'a few men at Somme and Ancre'. This, together with the centrality of a single character and the autobiographical element, might suggest a novel of adventure, whereas what Manning has written is a philosophical novel, in the sense of one which seeks to make

[89]

something of the war, to get beyond the sense of destruction which Aldington's work embodies. It is partly in this that the novel's nobility lies, but the idea of nobility is a troubling one.

One way of defining nobility would be to say that it occurs whenever humanity affirms humane values in the face of the anarchy of sense experience, while tragedy shows that the values may themselves be distorted or inadequate even while being noble. Letters from the front like the early efforts of Julian Grenfell may seem pitifully inadequate rather than tragic, but there is nobility in the effort to sustain the code which sent him there, just as, more generally, one can respond to the nobility of all those hopelessly immature subalterns who went to their deaths in defence of a code which necessitated those deaths. The danger in responding to such nobility is that the nobility itself may blind us to destructive systems. The Charge of the Light Brigade is almost the more heroic because of its futility – but it is dangerous to defend futility because it may highlight or inspire heroism.

What troubles me about *The Middle Parts of Fortune* is that it accepts war, and even in a sense glorifies it. More particularly, what is troubling is that Manning's intelligent and imaginative ability make the book plausible, even seductive. There is no cheap glorification: Manning is fully alert to the horrors of the First World War and to the strains it imposed: the opening makes this clear, as does the creation of the deserter, Miller, who comes and goes in the book, a disturbing revenant and sad reminder of how war can break a person. Manning, however, goes beyond suggesting that individuals can and do respond nobly to awful pressures, to imply that a profound peace may be achieved through the experience of war. Clearly,

[90]

anyone who is able to achieve this is to be admired, even envied, because such a person has found a way of continuing to face death and live. Such a person will have reached a position where she/he will not become one of those psychological cripples that recur in Aldington's pages. Moreover, because Manning is a real novelist, the resolution/return of Bourne does not seem faked as in Frankau, or made part of a wish-fulfilling vision as in Wells. Yet, in suggesting that the war provides Man's best opportunity to test and find himself, Manning gives war a valuable function in human life, and to that extent accepts war as not merely inevitable but glorious. Bourne's return to philosophical acceptance is fictionally convincing and satisfying – something is made from the experience. But human history is not only a record of defeat and failure. What achievements there have been have come from a refusal to accept that things like wars must happen. In a sense Manning's book – to an extent beyond Frankau, Bennett or Wells – makes the Great War tolerable, and that is both its achievement and its failure.

IV

The Novelist at Home

Lord Raingo and *Mr Britling* both make use of the
figure of the returning soldier partly to define the
consciousnesses of people at home, and there is clearly
a continuum from novels which use Home to point up
features of Front and those which reverse this process.
In this context 'home' is usually middle-class, public-
school and professional; an England seen with nostal-
gia and emphasis upon the idea of the country house.
The intrusion of the soldier upon this England can be
used to present a view of the impact of the war upon
those who take no direct part in it.

This is Rebecca West's concern in her short novel *The
Return of the Soldier,* which presents a young patrician
officer who copes with the war by developing amnesia.
The amnesia which Chris suffers arises less from any
specific sense of the enemy than from the strain of the
war as a whole, but West offers a bleak image of the
effects of international hostility. Chris rejects his wife
and home (and thus by implication his class and
upbringing) in his psychological effort to escape the
war. This suggests that he identifies the war less with
the Germans than with the English patrician class to
which he belongs. He turns back in his amnesia to the
lover of his very early adulthood, Margaret, who is his
social inferior and now a worn plebeian wife. It is

Margaret who brings Chris back from his amnesia, but this involves co-operating with those who are destroying Chris and so many others: 'he would go back to that flooded trench in Flanders under that sky more full of flying death than clouds . . .' (*Rebecca West: A Celebration*, Penguin, 1978, p. 67. *The Return of the Soldier* was first published in 1918).

West's novel suggests that the kind of England represented by Wells's Matching's Easy and, earlier, by Forster's Howard's End has responsibility for the war and, having allowed war, can only destroy its own. But Rudyard Kipling, in his story 'Mary Postgate', takes this analysis further. Mary is not herself patrician but she works for, and is approved of by, patricians. She is, in the words of Lady Causland's testimonial, 'thoroughly conscientious, tidy, companionable, and ladylike' (*A Diversity of Creatures*, 1917; *A Choice of Kipling's Prose*, Faber, 1987, p. 301). But she is also a middle-aged spinster who has identified strongly with her current employer's nephew, 'an unlovely orphan of eleven', who grows up treating her 'always as his butt and his slave' (p. 302). This Wyndham Fowler dies when he crashes on a Royal Flying Corps training flight. Later Mary, who has been dealing with his death with customary control and efficiency (significantly unable to weep) experiences the sight of the 'ripped and shredded body' of the young Edna Gerritt (p. 309) and decides, without evidence, that she is victim of a German air raid. When Mary, who is disposing of Wyndham's effects in the garden incinerator, comes across the figure of a fatally injured German airman she responds with cruelty rather than pity, watches him die in fear and pain, before returning for 'a luxurious hot bath' and coming down 'looking, as Miss Fowler said when she saw her lying all relaxed on the other sofa, "quite handsome" ' (p. 313).

Mary Postgate sees the German only as 'The thing beneath the oak' (p. 312). She cannot identify him with Wyndham, cannot even consider the evidence with regard to Edna. Instead she sees the cold supervision of the German's death as '*her* work . . . woman's work in the world' (p. 313). Mary is not broken by her experience, but rather draws strength from it. Kipling has stressed the implications of the Little Mother syndrome and Mary Postgate is a terrifying instance of the results of 'gross dichotomizing'.[1] A non-combatant, she contributes to war.

Wells's Mr Britling might be seen as a more comfortable representative of rural-genteel England, although he is perhaps less a character than an amalgam. Too old to fight in the war, he has a son, Hugh, who fights and dies, and whose letters tell us about the war at the front. Britling lives in the country as squire, a man of independent means. As a writer he is a popularizer and controversialist, and he is presented as having a wide variety of contacts, domestic, social, emotional and political. Since he is some sort of philosopher (albeit a mundane one) it is natural that he should constantly try to systematize experience as it happens, moving quickly, if not always consistently, from the particular to the general and showing a persistent desire to speculate from the present into the future. But Britling is a person to whom things happen: he does little except through his writing and he has little practical ability (as is suggested early in the novel by his incompetence with his car). Because of his age, his experience of the front is vicarious, coming to him through Hugh and Teddy, while his knowledge of the direct effects of German action on Britain comes through Aunt Wilshire. He wants to know and understand but, except emotionally, he meets the war mainly at second hand.

Mr Britling Sees It Through is very largely the story of the Britling consciousness, the material being filtered through Britling's mind and emotions and being organized by a mind used to analysis and theorizing. But it is important to make the point that Britling is a second-rate thinker, who can be seen as representative of Home response to the war. Britling undergoes typical experiences and responds typically. But modifications are called for. Britling is emphatically established as securely middle-class, and his range of responses is syncretic-reflective. The point about Britling's thinking is that it is neither original nor powerful: rather, he seems to draw together the responses of the thoughtful people of his class – so that it is wholly appropriate that *The Times* should be one of his outlets. Britling represents what typical men of his education, leisure and class thought about the war as it proceeded (or, more exactly, Wells's version of this). It should be added that Britling is modest enough – both in character and brain-power – to be able to change views as experience alters and accumulates. This capacity for change is indicated by what happens to Britling's writing in the course of the novel. At the beginning he is the confident producer of instant pamphlets; the man with ready and assured views about almost anything – with, it seems, the ambition to write a new *Arcadia*. As the book proceeds he has a period when his literary responses to experience become self-contradictory; he moves into silence; and emerges from silence into the final, tentative letter of self-questioning.

Wells, then, has created in Britling the sort of figure which allows him to write a novel of Britain-at-war while the war is still going on.[2] Britling's ability to alter his position allows Wells to suggest how responses in

Britain changed with events, and the same ability allows the novelist to indicate something of the difficulties of making up one's mind, particularly at second hand, about the nature of the war. Charles Edmonds – a combatant – wrote harshly of the book in his memoir, *A Subaltern's War* (1929). In Edmonds's view the novel should have been called 'Mr Wells does not see it through', 'since it reflected nothing but the weakening of the author's resolution':

> Mr Britling entered upon the war period in a heroic spirit which lasted just so long as he imagined that war meant victory without sacrifice. Confronted by the calamities and misfortunes of 1916, Mr Britling lost his nerve and became a flabby and verbose 'défaitiste', not a true pacifist, merely a man who thought that fine words would solve practical problems. (Peter Davies, p. 93)

This is a mixture of justice and unfairness. Britling *is* verbose and he does tend to take a sanguine view of the efficacy of words. Moreover, he is inclined to allow linguistic facility to lead him to unjustified optimism. But it is less fair to say that Britling loses his nerve: his view of the war changes, but he continues, on the whole, to face facts and to try to make sense of them, although clearly not the sense Edmonds approves of. Edmonds also assumes that Wells and Britling are, or amount to, the same thing, a critical heresy which, however, does glance at one of the unsatisfactory aspects of the novel.

Since Britling lives through the war, has representative experiences, and seeks to make sense of them, Wells's novel is, among other things, an anthology of national attitudes to the war as featured in the popular imagination at home – the Irish question, the matter of Belgian neutrality, German atrocities, Zeppelin raids,

[96]

the American attitude to participation, and so on. Much of the interest of *Mr Britling Sees It Through* lies in Wells's account of such issues, but this feature of the novel also creates problems, for Britling is almost inevitably an evasive figure. Somers, in Lawrence's *Kangaroo* (see p. 111), is fiercely individualistic and responds to the war with all the conviction of an outsider who sees himself as heroic to the point of martyrdom. Hoape, in Bennett's *The Pretty Lady* (see p. 100), is more representative, but he is given an active, if secondary role in the war effort and he lives in London, firmly at the centre of the domestic war. But Britling, while formally an individual, is both everything and nothing. He looks suspiciously like a figure created to allow Wells to touch on anything he wants without too much difficulty or coherence: Britling's war is neither 'One Man's Initiation' (the title of Dos Passos's first novel) nor 'Pilgrim's Progress', and as a result there is neither the intensity of a Somers nor the near allegorical status of Williamson's Bullock.

This can be put another way, by saying that it is difficult to feel sure about Wells's attitude to his character. Certainly, Britling is no simple double for Wells, who stands at some ironic distance from his character, but it is not always easy to see how far this irony is meant to go nor how we are to read it. Britling is often a mildly comic figure, and there is no necessary contradiction between a figure being both faintly absurd and fundamentally sympathetic (Wells himself succeeded with this blend in *Kipps*). But are we to see Britling as a man who 'sees it through' by indulging his own capacity for inconsistency, or is he meant to seem admirably open-minded and honest in his responses, showing the generosity of spirit which might prevent recurrence of war? Is his final sense of 'Wave after wave

[97]

of warmth and light' to be seen as a reassuring vision or as sentimental delusion? The questions are easier to ask than answer. Wells has a basically detached manner, the ironies allowing him avenues of retreat, but the result in this novel is an unconvincing mixture of local commitments and overall vagueness of purpose, whereby Wells seems a good-hearted but wet liberal.

Oddly, since Britling (like Wells himself) has the desire to synthesize, the novel seems finally to want to avoid any marked conclusions, which is understandable, since the war was still going on. Britling's changes of view (however locally plausible) add up to a postponement of real analysis, so that the novel begins to look like a personal documentary without any consistent angle of presentation. It cannot have such an angle because Britling himself is a character who is incapable of achieving one – he has plurality of viewpoint, and Wells does not finally convince us that this is either an inevitable result of a complex personality responding to complex experience or an ironized account of an inadequate character. It seems, then, that Wells himself is unaware that humorous irony is not ultimately enough, and Edmonds's adjectives come to seem fair, if unkind. Such irony is inadequate in *Mr Britling Sees It Through* because it fails to mask or confront the sentimental view that nothing basic needs to be changed, or can be changed. The novel begins with a vision of bucolic England, invaded only by comic motor cars, and it purports to show how this England is tested by the war. Yet, although Wells's England is challenged by the war – from the German coastal raids to the death of Hugh and presumed death of Teddy – we end with a vision of a bucolic future. We, as readers, might wonder whether this could be meant as the final indictment of Britling himself, but there is little reason to think that

Wells means this. It seems, rather, that we are to feel that Britling has undergone the dark night of the soul and that from his agony he has emerged a better and wiser man. Yet this wisdom is, to put it mildly, insubstantial, consisting only of the sentimental proposition that 'Our sons have shown us God . . .' (p. 269) and the vision of light and warmth over Matching's Easy. If we ask of the novel what God has been shown us, or how the revelation is to be applied in our mundane lives, we get no answer: and if we look, in the years since 1918, for evidence of warmth and light we find little of either, especially if we do not live in Matching's Easy. It might then be said that the end of the novel is less an indictment of Britling than of his creator.

The lack of substance in Wells's ending may be linked to the fact that his novel was written before the end of the war, but the effort to provide a vision of light and, therefore, hope also suggests that *Mr Britling* functions partly as propaganda. Britling can be seen as a person of modest abilities and moral quality. He is certainly no Richard Hannay – but Britling 'sees it through'. He has faced loss and repeated blows to his psyche, but, at the end, he is still functioning, still able to think and, most importantly, still able to look forward with real, if imprecise, optimism. The war will not be a waste. Wells might have seen such an ending as part of his responsibility as a writer: he might even have hoped that it would help to make a positive future possible.

Arnold Bennett's *The Pretty Lady* begins in the theatre, this being seen in the manner of Zola's *Nana*:

> The stage scene flamed extravagantly with crude orange and viridian light, a rectangle of bedazzling illumination; on the boards, in the midst of great width,

[99]

with great depth behind them and arching height above, tiny squeaking figures ogled the primeval passion in gesture and innuendo.

The sexual emphasis here reflects the reality of the whoredom of the Promenade – 'Behind the audience came the restless Promenade, where was the reality which the stage reflected ((1918) Cassell, 1932, p. 14) – and it is only at the end of the brief opening chapter that the war is hinted at, with the reference to 'the vivid courtesans and their clientèle in black, tweed, or khaki' (pp. 14–15).

By the end of the novel, however, the Great War has become the central concern of Bennett's male protagonist, G. J. Hoape:

> He stood still, and the vast sea of war seemed to be closing over him. The war was growing, or the sense of its measureless scope was growing. It had sprung, not out of this crime or that, but out of the secret invisible roots of humanity, and it was widening to the limits of evolution itself . . . (p. 314)

This contrast suggests the way in which *The Pretty Lady* becomes a novel about the war, but it is more accurate to speak of it as a novel set in the period of the war, and perhaps most accurate to say that *The Pretty Lady* is a social novel which uses the war to further analysis of aspects of English society.

The 'pretty lady' of Bennett's title is the French courtesan Christine Dubois. Zola had seen Nana as representing the decadence of the society which produced her and in which she flourishes for a while: Nana is both victim and predator. Christine, however, is not precisely either a victim of the war, or a product of the world at war. She is 'the accidental daughter of a daughter of joy', product of the profession to which she

[100]

herself comes to belong, and introduced to it by her own mother, who 'Actuated by deep maternal solicitude . . . brought her daughter back to Paris, and had her inducted into the profession under the most decent auspices' (p. 21). Christine's profession makes her vulnerable and fairly rootless. Prostitutes live in society's shadows, neither accepted nor rejected, used by males who find it virtually impossible either to recognize them or do without them. The war provides, in Bennett's view, opportunities for Christine and her sisters, while also exacerbating their vulnerability. It is the war which sends Christine to London from Paris, via Belgium, and we shall see that she is harmed by the war.

Christine is not particularly intelligent, and Bennett's presentation of her is annoyingly banal in several respects, but both her foreignness and her profession make her an important element in the novel's account of English society. In this society, at least at its upper levels, a man like Hoape can make habitual use of prostitutes and may even form a strong emotional attachment to one, but the relationship must be largely covert, conducted in private and on the social fringes represented by the Promenade and night clubs. Christine may be 'put among her own furniture' but only once visits Hoape's apartment and could never be part of his public life. Such a society is obviously living a lie. Moreover, it is a society which is shown to be not very good at coping with the war. Christine is deeply ignorant about the war, but she at least performs a useful service by providing sexual satisfaction for officers (private soldiers, of course, have to make do with street-walkers). In society there are Queen and Con. Queen plays at war work, indulging herself with no real sense of service, and her death on the roof of

Lechford House is the appropriate result of her grotesque triviality and folly. Con is better than this: her period in Glasgow (even if marked by attitudinizing) seems a genuine effort to serve and to recognize the sacrifices made by many women outside her own class. But Con lacks the mental balance to make any true contribution: her breakdown on her first appearance as secretary to the executive committee of the Lechford hospitals marks her lack of stamina (rooted, ironically, in the death of her husband at the front). There is a striking contrast between Con and Queen, on the one hand, and such plebeians as Mrs Braiding and Nurse Smaith on the other – to say nothing of the Glasgow munitions girls.

Christine's ability to make a success of genteel prostitution and, more specifically, her attraction for Hoape, indicate the limitations of such women as Queen and Con. Hoape has some awareness that they offer less than full satisfaction, and he not only sees Queen's posturings for what they are but is also aware of Con's theatricality. And although Bennett fails to get very far into the psyche of a Christine, he avoids making her a simple golden-hearted whore, being alert to her over-sensitivity, vanity and greed. Society's hypocrisy and dishonesty make a Christine, and it is this same society which runs the war. Bennett's chief example is G. J. Hoape.

Hoape is the only major character who operates in both Christine's world and in that of Queen and Con. Too old to fight, he drifts into war work. A wealthy bachelor, he tends to relate the war to his own needs and interests. By instinct he sees the enlistment of his servant Braiding in terms of the threat this offers to his own comfort and the war in terms of what it offers him. His money comes from industry, but he is an investor rather than an industrialist and he has no interest in how industry works or in the conditions of industrial workers, even of those in factories from which his dividends come. At the novel's start, Hoape is essentially functionless, socially useful only in that the exercise of his moneyed leisure provides employment for club servants, domestics – and whores. The war improves Hoape's dividends, and here again he profits from the labour of others, but it also gives him an active function and, with it, greater confidence in his abilities, thus making him a civilian parallel to Forester's Curzon. Increased involvement in his work with the Lechford hospitals leads to greater fulfilment. Hoape is properly critical of the selfish war work of such as Queen, but the limits of his own service are marked in several ways. He makes no discernible sacrifice: his committee work simply gives him something to do and salves his conscience, without requiring any real sacrifice of leisure. Moreover, there is the gap between his commitment and that of such as Nurse Smaith, who is directly involved in helping war casualties, and the Glasgow munitions workers, directly involved in producing the weapons of war. There is also a contrast between Hoape, the comfortable civilian lover of Christine, and the alcoholic soldier she sentimentally befriends.

Hoape is complacent at the start and never really breaks out of this state. He deals with Con's account of the reality of Glasgow by reducing it to her mental instability, and his own sensitivity is severely limited. One of the best passages in the novel is the incident of the air raid (chapters 29, 30) in which Bennett captures, quite brilliantly, the shock and panic which the raid produces. As Hoape looks for Christine in the aftermath he realizes that he has dropped his stick, and he looks for it with his torch:

The sole object of interest which the torch revealed was a
child's severed arm, with a fragment of brown frock on it
and a tinsel ring on one of the fingers of the dirty little
hand. The blood from the other end had stained the
ground. G. J. abruptly switched off the torch. Nausea
overcame him, and then a feeling of the most intense pity
and anger overcame the nausea. (A month elapsed before
he could mention the discovery of the child's arm to
anyone at all.) (p. 208)

The quality of this emerges in the contrast between the
cool 'sole object of interest' and the nature of the object
itself; in the restraint of the detail; in the confidence to
leave the incident isolated from the rest of the narrative; and in what it suggests about Hoape. Hoape would
indeed be callous if he were not made nauseous by the
incident, and it is hardly surprising that he suppresses
it for a month, or that, after nausea, he should feel pity
and anger. But the detail of the arm remains isolated
not only from the main narrative but also from Hoape's
responses to the war, for his pity and anger go
nowhere. They do not alter his conduct to any discernible extent and they have no serious long-term effects
upon his sensibility.

Bennett is coolly precise about Hoape, particularly at
the novel's end. Certainly, Hoape is presented as
becoming more aware of the war as the novel progresses and he does come to a sense of it which takes him
outside himself, to some extent, most evidently in the
closing passages. He also sees that Queen – 'courting
destruction, and being destroyed' – can be seen as a
symbol of a society in collapse. At the same time,
however, he thinks of Con as a symbol of civilization's
'nobility and its elements of reason' (p. 315) – and this
is tricky. Bennett is presenting this as Hoape's own
reflection and one can see what is meant by Con's

nobility, but she is deeply unstable (her instability being either the result of the war, or at least exacerbated by it) and if she represents salvation we need to remember that, on her last appearance, she is speaking of suicide. And the presented facts continue to throw doubt on Hoape's judgement, right to the novel's end. He sees himself as having 'discovered in the war a task which suited his powers, which was genuinely useful' (p. 315) – but there is little sign that he is aware of the complacency of this or of his thankfulness 'that he had a balanced and sagacious mind, and could judge justly' (p. 315). For Hoape fails to judge either Christine or himself justly.

Put crudely, Hoape fails to estimate Christine as a human being. Paradoxically, he continues to see her as essentially a whore, yet finally rejects her for being one. In a sense this is fair enough since Christine shows the same confusion. She is, in her own estimation, not even really a courtesan; has a horror of ending on the streets; cannot bring herself to accept that she is a prostitute. But Christine is responding to a society which created her: she has little of Hoape's freedom and nothing of his class-given power to shape society. At best, like Nana, she has to work insidiously. Hoape, therefore, must bear the greater responsibility for self-deception, and the closing section of *The Pretty Lady* shows how little he has learnt, even in the exceptional circumstances of the war.

Bennett's novel presents society in time of war on two levels. The more public of these is the home society of the first chapter, and this is best represented by Queen. In Bennett's first chapter the febrile, superficial world of West End revue is only slightly disturbed by the mention of khaki, but that world at large – represented by Queen's theatricals, by Lechford House

[105]

and Hoape's club – is, for the reader, radically disturbed on several occasions – by the child's arm, by Nurse Smaith, by the alcoholic soldier, and by the scalp of the munitions worker. Yet, despite Con's sensitivity to her Glasgow experience and Hoape's pain and anger at the child's arm, the social world in this novel remains largely impervious to these disturbances, disturbances which spring from the war's reality. The Marquis of Lechford may be rendered helpless by the coroner at the inquest on Queen, but there is no sign that he and his like will ever be aware of what is involved while wire netting designed to protect Lechford House from aerial bombardment stops short of the servants' quarters.

At times Bennett makes his points brilliantly in *The Pretty Lady*. He uses theatricality well: it leads from the theatre itself to the Promenade (professional drama to professional sex) to Queen (an amateur performer at art and life) and to Con (whose account of her Glasgow experience strikes Hoape as performance). And he uses nudity even better. The 'half-clad lovely' of the revue (p. 13) links with the exploitation of nakedness in prostitution, but also with the display of Queen's Salome dance. And all this titillation is finely placed by the full and functional nudity of the female workers in Glasgow, who have to strip bare for safety at work.

These motifs obviously put pressure on the society which is central to the novel, providing a dramatized criticism of the failure of the privileged to understand the war's ubiquity and significance. Con is the only one among the privileged who seems truly able to *feel* the war, and this destroys her. But Bennett backs the public drama with a more private one, wherein the war fails to lead Hoape to any full understanding of the world which he exploits. Hoape's final reflections are of

[106]

little use, for they include sentimentality towards Con, injustice to Christine and complacency to himself. How, then, can they even begin to embrace the terrible details of the child's arm and worker's scalp? *The Pretty Lady* tells us nothing directly about the battlefields, but Bennett's version of the home front is a depressing commentary on futility.

The Pretty Lady can be seen as a study of its protagonist, G. J. Hoape, and, through him, of the type of society he comes from and exemplifies. Hoape is a broadly representative character and, although Bennett clearly has a sense of history, he is less interested in how the society he is concerned with came to be as it is than with its nature and performance in the particular circumstances of the war. Also, Bennett is not particularly interested in how the war came about, whereas D. H. Lawrence, in *Kangaroo,* concerns himself with the war as product of processes anterior to it. Like Aldington, Lawrence sees the roots of the war in political rather than social terms, for while he comments on 'the German military creatures' – 'mechanical bullies they were' (*Kangaroo* (1923), Penguin, 1950, p. 237) – his main concern is with the war as an expression of a process by which patriotism and democracy have become identified with industrialism and commercialism. *Kangaroo* is not a programmatic novel but is concerned with the destruction of an 'old England' which is to be seen as an England of the 'aristocratic principle', and it is tempting to see this as similar to Yeats's engagement with country houses and to tie it up with Aldington's belief in the value of rooted landed families. But Lawrence's aristocracy, in novels prior to *Kangaroo*, had been less a presentation of the landed class as such than a concern with hierarchical traditions throughout society and with the destruction of such traditions by industrialization. Aristocracy, for Lawrence, is less a matter of birth than nature: his aristocrats include the Brangwens of the opening pages of *The Rainbow* (1915) and, later, the gypsy of *The Virgin and the Gypsy* (1929). Birth (in the sense of social privilege) is of coincidental relevance only. Such aristocracy is seen as threatened by industrialization, and in *The Rainbow* and *Women in Love* Lawrence is concerned with the destruction of rooted, cyclic nature, culture and society by the forces of industrial materialism.

Such industrialism ruins landscapes, but Lawrence is less concerned with this kind of vandalism than with what this suggests about the ruining of mankind's relationship with nature, a relationship which is more impressive when seen as organic – in, for instance, the superb opening chapter of *The Rainbow* – than in the more technical terms of the late essay 'Nottingham and the Mining Countryside'. And it seems that Lawrence is not opposed to industrialism as such but to what, in his understanding, it signifies. What this entails is, above all, greed and the loss of individual integrity. Such greed is not merely expressed by industrialists themselves but also by workers, and one of its expressions is democracy. A narrow and greedy concern with the material leads, so Lawrence suggests, to the denial of the need for inequality. The mass, with greedy and purblind selfishness, denies its natural leaders; while (with equivalent blindness) these leaders renege on the responsibilities which are their privilege. Democracy is the refusal to accept the need for the leadership principle: industrialization is indicted because it facilitates such refusal by shattering traditions based on that principle and encourages society's leaders to focus on materialism rather than on fostering hierarchical responsibility.

Lawrence's concern with the effects of industrialization links him with a major preoccupation of the English novel in the nineteenth century. Both Dickens and Elizabeth Gaskell are involved with the issues raised by England's rapid industrial growth. They both, however, write with a sense that industrialization is a process which is still in progress and they are alert to its potential good as well as to its evils. Hardy creates a Wessex which is marked by intimations of the Industrial Revolution and which is facing crisis, but Hardy is very much aware that movement from the pastoral to the industrial is far from complete.[3] Lawrence, however, writes as if the process is essentially over, or, at least, as if the decisive moment has passed. Only the full working out remains, and to change what has taken place will require revolution. In *Kangaroo* Lawrence sees the war as a logical consequence of the drift to industrial democracy, and the war is also marked by the denial of individuality. This is sometimes seen in terms of a 'they' who oppress Somers – 'How they tried, with their beastly industrial self-righteousness, to humiliate him as a separate, single man . . .' (p. 237) – but it is also a matter of individuals betraying themselves: '. . . in every country practically every man lost his head, and lost his own centrality, his own manly isolation in his own integrity, which alone keeps life real' (p. 236).

But if the war is the logical climax of the drift to industrialization it is necessary to notice that Lawrence sees the war as actively contributing to enactment of the drift itself, for industrial democracy is not seen simply as expressing itself through the war but as taking advantage of an opportunity provided by the

[109]

war to further its cause. Lawrence identifies the climax/crisis specifically with Lloyd George's ministry. By implication, at least, Asquith, his predecessor, is seen as a leader in the tradition, as the last representative of the aristocratic past, while Lloyd George is, for Lawrence, the voice of the 'criminal public', personification of the forces of industrialization and commercialization, which 'during the later years of the war' steadily applied torture 'to break the independent soul in any man who would not hunt with the criminal mob' (p. 235). This associates Asquith with independence and Lloyd George with the mob.

Lawrence's account has less to do with politics as usually understood than with a kind of psycho-politics. He makes no effort, for example, to rebut contemporary criticism of Asquith as a lazily inefficient and backwards-looking war-leader, nor is he interested in giving Lloyd George credit for his energy and conviction as a prime minister in war-time. Such a discussion would be beside his point. The suggestion is that an Asquith would not produce war, while a Lloyd George does. This is historical nonsense, but, by pinning the social crisis to the Lloyd George government, Lawrence can both present this as the product of industrial democracy and also focus the crisis upon those-who-stayed-at-home: 'all the stay-at-home bullies who governed the country during those years' (p. 235).[4] What is suggested is that such elements in society as might have prevented or delayed crisis went, because of their quality, to the front, while those who did not go were the typical second-raters to whom democracy panders. This allows Lawrence to utilize the widespread resentment felt by officers and men at the front towards those who were still at home. One of the forms such resentment takes is the belief that the breakdown of relationships between

[110]

home and front necessitates some form of revolution. More exactly, the appropriate context for Lawrence's view of the implications of this breakdown is provided by those revolutions-to-the-right which Robert Wohl has written about (in *The Generation of 1914,* Weidenfeld and Nicolson, 1980). But it is also important, as should become clear, to stress that Lawrence sees the war as produced by those who did not fight in it.

For reasons which relate to Lawrence's own life the real war in *Kangaroo* is fought at home (see Paul Delaney, *D. H. Lawrence's Nightmare,* Harvester, 1979). As with the lack of interest in orthodox politics, Lawrence's avoidance of details of fighting at the front is a statement of where he felt the significant struggle lay. Front fighting is secondary to the real issue, of which it is the product, and the vital matter is the war between the 'criminal public', the hyenas, the 'canaille', and 'the independent soul'.

In *Kangaroo* this soul is Richard Somers, and chapter 12 ('The Nightmare') is an account of the testing of Somers by the 'criminal public'. Somers is not against war as such – 'he had no conscientious objection to war' (p. 236) – but against the spirit of this war – 'the vast mob-spirit, which he could never acquiesce in' (p. 236) – a spirit which is the product of industrial democracy. Somers's main charge is that the spirit of the war, more especially as summed up in the Lloyd George war, is determined to break independent souls through humiliation and intimidation. Lawrence writes impressively of the torment which Somers feels at his medical examination, and such passages present Somers as a figure analogous to Christ on his journey to Calvary. Like Christ at that climactic stage of his mission, Somers is isolated, but Lawrence is at pains to suggest that Somers is no freak. He is only isolated, while recognizing similar individuality in others, because of the degree to which he takes his resistance and his understanding of why it is necessary to resist.

Somers comes to see that the old England is doomed and that he must escape. This leads him to Australia – and back to the consequences of the war. Somers's Australia is both very old and very young. It is young in terms of European culture, and specifically in terms of European industrial democracy. But this youthfulness is itself European and is expressed distastefully in the casual detritus of cans and bottles, a scurf which demonstrates the promiscuous irresponsibility which Lawrence associates with democracy. Yet this Australian youthfulness also gives Somers grounds for hope in that it suggests to him that democratic degeneracy has not reached in Australia the advanced stage found in England. This is also hopeful because the new degeneracy has not yet covered or diseased the old Australia. The naked, aboriginal quality of that country has still not been wholly masked by 'civilization', and so the Dark Gods are more accessible there. The tension between the aboriginal and the civilized in *Kangaroo* is, of course, a motif of much of Lawrence's later writing (notably in *The Plumed Serpent* and *St Mawr*) but in *Kangaroo* the tension is presented in a way which leads back to the Great War. Somers, drawn to contemplate and participate in the war between aboriginal Australia and the younger presence of imported industrial democracy, is brought face to face with consequences of the Great War, in ways which make it clear why, in chapter 12, Lawrence is anxious to differentiate between those who fought and those who did not.

Somers is not alone in feeling that democracy is a perversion. Through his neighbour, Jack, he comes in contact with the Diggers, men who share Somers's hatred of what has happened in England and of what is threatening Australia. These men are mainly ex-soldiers, and it is their experience of the disciplined adherence to leadership which has 'made' them and led to their recognition of the wrongness of democracy. War has been creative for these men; and their war at the front, while being the product of democracy, has not in itself tainted them. Lawrence's Diggers are his vision of those societies of former soldiers touched on in an earlier chapter, and Somers's contact with them reduces his sense of isolation.

But Lawrence is not a fantasist of Wells's type, and *Kangaroo* is a novel of lessons not fully learnt. Somers cannot fully identify with the Diggers because they – and most importantly Kangaroo himself – fail to respond fully to the importance of the Dark Gods. The Diggers are still too much wedded to politics as usually understood, and as such are figures who do not understand the need for that break with civilization which Somers sees as fundamental to the regeneration of Man. Until there is such understanding even a Kangaroo will continue to be perverse and Somers will remain isolated, a kind of Christ as Wandering Jew.

In so far as, for Lawrence, the war was a catalyst, it marked both the cataclysmic confluence of tendencies, which he regarded as disastrous for Man, and the opportunity to destroy those tendencies. He makes it clear, however, that the opportunity provided by the war was, in his view, seized within the period of the war itself by the 'criminal public'. It is post-war that allows those who have come to understand the nature of the war the chance of realigning the dominant mode of human existence. The war, so far as *Kangaroo* is concerned, was a 'terrible, terrible war' (p. 236) because of its denial of individual integrity, but it did teach

[113]

lessons to those who would learn, and even if the Diggers are seen as not learning enough the novel ends with Somers still alive. It is not so important to resist Lawrence's view of history as to resist his view of the lessons of history. But it is also important to respond to *Kangaroo*'s account of how the Great War in many ways revealed not humankind's finest qualities but its worst – the intolerance of dissent, the tyranny of nationalism, the brutality of bullying. One does not have to be entirely sympathetic either to Somers or to Lawrence himself to be properly ashamed of what happened to minorities in England during the war.[5]

Richard Aldington remained angry to the end of his life that the war destroyed so much and improved so little, while the Lawrence of *Kangaroo* feels both anger at what the war seemed to show about our civilization and some sort of hope that out of the crisis might come a revolution. Manning, largely free of anger, draws stoic optimism from Bourne's experiences, while Williamson, in *The Patriot's Progress*, at least shows awareness of a crisis arising from the way in which the war played upon the sensibility of his central character. Wells is evasive, for while it is plausible that Britling finds consolation in his soft, wet God, this is an unconvincing conclusion – the final second-rate synthesis of a second-rate thinker whose relation to his creator is as imprecise as his relation to his Creator. At least C. R. Bensted saw that Warne's sort of Anglicanism would no longer do.

V

Roots and Uprootings

The Great War has much to do with land, as dirt and as
nation. Britain entered the war when German troops
violated the declared and guaranteed neutrality of
Belgium in order to move quickly on to French soil. In
the fighting vast areas of land were occupied by troops,
while the traditional occupiers became refugees. Germans and German-descendants living in Britain were
taken from their 'land' and interned. The British royal
family uprooted its German family name and replaced
it with an English one. At the front soldiers dug
themselves into the earth, uprooted themselves for
attacks, or were uprooted by shells or mines. Buildings
were ripped away from their foundations and families
were ripped apart. Many people (not only combatants)
were more subtly deracinated by the experience of war,
their social, cultural, even geographical roots damaged.
Ivor Gurney is perhaps one of the saddest examples of
this, but there were many others. The theme of roots
and kinds of uprooting was a rich one and two novelists
of the war – R. H. Mottram and Ford Madox Ford –
treated it with particular fullness.

Mottram published three novels about the war
between 1924 and 1926. They were called *The Spanish
Farm, Sixty-Four, Ninety-Four,* and *The Crime at
Vanderlynden's,* and they were republished as a trilogy

in 1927, when three short pieces ('D'Archeville', 'The Winner' and 'The Stranger') were added to form links between the originally separate novels. In addition Mottram also wrote several short stories using the figures of Skene and Dormer from the novels, these appearing in *Ten Years Ago* (1928; 'forming a pendant to the Spanish Farm Trilogy'). Taken as a whole this material represents a long attempt to describe the war, perhaps the most ambitious in English fiction.

Part of this ambition may be seen in Mottram's attempt to render several centres of consciousness. Most English novels of the war use a single central consciousness or a group one, but Mottram attempts a greater range. Skene and Dormer are from the same town and socially very similar, but the first of the novels centres upon the French peasant woman Madeleine, while the links focus on a French aristocrat, a Canadian officer and the generalized figure simply called 'The Stranger'. What is most important here is the use of Madeleine in *The Spanish Farm,* for the nature and behaviour of the peasant woman, especially in relation to Skene, are important aspects of Mottram's treatment of rootedness. It is worth mentioning that there are other quite extended treatments of French women in English fiction of the war (notably in Bennett's *The Pretty Lady* and Ford's *The Last Post*); but Mottram is perhaps unique in presenting such a figure on her own territory.

The treatment of territory in Mottram's trilogy is closely connected with the treatment of time. The antiquity of the Spanish Farm itself is stressed, as is the earlier presence of British troops in this Flemish landscape, while the novels play across the time-span of the war itself, stressing both the breaks between pre-war and war and sub-divisions within the war period.

Also, and this is especially true if the pendant *Ten Years Ago* is taken into account, Mottram is concerned with the immediate post-war period. Skene, Dormer, Madeleine and D'Archeville are all young adults, but Mottram's world also has a number of important older figures – Jerome Vanderlynden, the senior D'Archevilles and, in the short stories, a series of old peasants. Interestingly, there are no children of importance: none of the chief protagonists has a child, and in that sense the trilogy offers no future.

'A farmer stood watching a battalion of infantry filing into his pasture.' These are the opening words of *The Spanish Farm*. In the course of the trilogy reference is made to many visits to the farm, by many soldiers, while Mottram is concerned to stress the durability and permanence of the farm buildings. Edmund Blunden wrote a number of fine poems about ways in which the war destroyed buildings and a theme of the revisiting stories in *Ten Years Ago* is the way in which shelling and reclamation have made territory unrecognizable. But the farm is not destroyed, even though it is damaged, and it endures, a product of the past. It is also, it seems, an international product:

> The farmer wore a Dutch cap, spoke Flemish by preference, but could only write French. His farm was called Ferme 1' Espagnole – The Spanish Farm – and stood on French soil. (p. 3. My references are all to the *Spanish Farm Trilogy, 1914–1918*, Chatto and Windus, 1927.)

The soldiers who are filing in at the novel's beginning are British and the British have been here before. So Kavanagh tells Dormer of the 'little old medieval walled town' which is 'for the third time in its history garrisoned by an English army' (p. 719). The farm is dated to 1610 (p. 256) and another farm 'reminded Skene of Spanish Farm. It was, in fact, another of that chain of farm-fortresses left by Alva, three hundred years ago' (p. 329). The farm and the territory around it are palimpsests, written on by fighting and cultivation for several centuries, but they are also palimpsests in being written on within the history of the war by the movements of troops and peasants. Madeleine, Jerome and the elder Vanderlynden sister come and go, but the farm remains and the ways of life associated with it endure. The 'Mairie of Haagedoorne', like the farm itself, 'had seen soldiers in its four hundred years, had been built for Spanish ones, and had seen them replaced by French and Dutch, English and Hessians' (p. 568), but Flanders is a land of 'undisturbed rusticity', and Madeleine is seen as the essence of the farm and its land:

> For she was the Spanish Farm, the implacable spirit of that borderland so often fought over, never really conquered. (p. 234)

The making of the farm, then, has an international dimension and in the course of the war, we are told, 'practically the whole English Army must have passed through or near it at one time or another' (p. 13). Contact between races, therefore, is marked, and this is most strongly shown in the relationship between Skene and Madeleine. The latter, as we learn early in *The Spanish Farm,* is the lover of the young D'Archeville, a local aristocrat now serving in the war. During the period of the trilogy Madeleine and Skene become lovers and, although D'Archeville is killed, the Flemish peasant and the English architect-soldier survive.

[118]

We are not, however, encouraged to make much of the relationship of Skene and Madeleine. The passage which ends *The Spanish Farm* and which invokes Madeleine as the spirit of Flanders contains disturbing notes. Madeleine 'was perhaps the most concrete expression of humanity's instinctive survival in spite of its own perversity and ignorance', but, Mottram goes on, 'There must she stand, slow-burning revenge incarnate, until a better, gentler time' (p. 234). Revenge for what? And when will a 'better, gentler time' come?

There are moments in the trilogy when identity is emphasized, as here:

> From the extemporized mess to the farmer's part of the house, was like stepping from modern war into a Yorkshire farmhouse of the eighteenth century. (p. 268)

But Mottram sees contact as superficial: 'It was England, simply a piece of English life cut neatly out and pasted on the map of Flanders' (p. 324). The English have come again to Flanders, but they pass through and will go. So Skene comes to realize that Madeleine 'did not want him, had never wanted him, nor any Englishman, nor anything English. He was just one of the things the War, the cursed War, had brought on her, and now it, and they, were going . . . The only thing she and Skene had in common, was the War. The War removed, they had absolutely no means of contact. Their case was not isolated. It was national' (p. 233). The trilogy shows much tolerant amity, but little understanding, and the revisitings of *Ten Years Ago* are all failures of contact and recognition. Madeleine's vengefulness is not simply directed at the Germans or any other race. Instead it is a matter of the desire for revenge against everything which has, in her view, cheated her and hers in the war. Hers is a narrow, self-interested vengefulness, the product of the death of her lover, the destruction of her father and the damage done to the farm. Her spirit does not compromise.

The land of Flanders, it seems, however much it is torn, returns to itself and its roots, essentially unchanged. None of the English remain, though some may revisit. Separation is the keynote. The love-making of Madeleine and Skene is not made cheap by this, but is only significant within the context of the war. This all sounds bleak enough, and Mottram's version of the end of the war is hardly encouraging. D'Archeville is dead, as is the Canadian 'uncle', and sad incidental corpses inevitably fill the record. Madeleine endures, without a lover and with a father made a zombie by his experience of the war. Skene has survived, but he has been drastically disturbed:

> Homewards!
> But in his heart was a nasty qualm, a feeling that he was not really going home, that home lay behind him, in the rough-and-ready, meagre-hearty 'mess' – even further, in some well-groomed graveyard on the Belgium frontier . . . (p. 553)

Skene goes back to his home town and pre-war occupation, but *Ten Years Ago* presents him as unassimilated. All he shares are the common experiences with Dormer. For his part, the latter, who, unlike Skene, has made no significant contact with the French, sees the end of the war as escape:

> . . . ahead was visible the moderately white cliffs of England . . . This last passage of the Channel was, this time, real escape. The Crime at Vanderlynden's was behind him. He had got away from it at last. (p. 786)

This crime at the Spanish Farm had been one of contact, or non-contact, the violation of a Catholic shrine, more from carelessness than motives of sacrilege. It represents quite well the lack of understanding, the essential separateness, which is one of Mottram's main themes, but it has also been the bane of Dormer's life in the army, and he is escaping this also.

Both in the trilogy and in several places in *Ten Years Ago* Mottram sees the Armistice as anti-climax. For Madeleine the end simply means that the shells stop and the damage is left (p. 221). An anonymous figure, 'plodding beside a somnambulistic horse', at the end of the chapter called 'Victory' in *Sixty-Four, Ninety-Four,* has a brief exchange with Skene. On being told that the Germans are about to sign Armistice terms this figure merely remarks 'Good job. We should have chucked it, if they hadn't!', and Skene reflects that the war has gone on too long:

> 'Who cares now?'
> He had forgotten that this was Victory. (p. 535)

A captain in *The Crime at Vanderlynden's* echoes this figure and, we are told, voices Dormer's own view when he says, 'I believe, in another week, we'd have had both sides simply laying down their arms' (p. 771). The view of the soldiers is that there is nothing to celebrate. The war has just exhausted itself. There is nothing in *Ten Years Ago* to suggest that Mottram saw the aftermath any differently.

Mottram is not unusual in viewing the Armistice as anti-climax, so far as the troops are concerned, nor is he unusual in emphasizing that reassimilation of the troops after the war was difficult. There is little of the bitterness in his account which we find in Aldington, in

Sassoon's poems and in Remarque's *The Road Back,* but the alienation is there. Yet Mottram does not present either a revolutionary or a particularly pessimistic account.

We have noticed that, at the end of his novel *Le Feu* (*Under Fire*), Henri Barbusse offered a vision of international socialism as hope for the future. His optimism is put in perspective by the corresponding vision of another French novelist, Jules Romains, whose *Verdun* was published in 1938, on the edge of another world war. Like Mottram, Romains sees the end of the Great War as characterized by exhaustion. In fact he provides an even more negative ending, since he sees the war as simply fragmenting into marauding bands of outlaws, this being a grim version of the theme of comradeship. For Romains the war lapses into a past before the formation of nations, but in Mottram neither collapse nor revolution is envisaged. How these are avoided takes us back to Skene and Dormer.

Not only are they from the same town, they have similar backgrounds and similar jobs (Skene as an architect, Dormer as a bank clerk). Both are middle-rank officers; both are volunteers; both mix active service with administrative military functions. Neither is particularly gregarious and both are given to reflection. Both think well of the 'other ranks', but neither is seen as particularly inward with private soldiers. Their perspectives are of the modest provincial middle class. Both are seen as decent men who do their best in the war, without enjoying it or seeking to do any great damage to others. Neither shows any phobic dislike of Germans or any strong antipathy to the French. In the trilogy there is little to suggest that Skene and Dormer know each other, but the stories of *Ten Years Ago* present them as at least acquaintances:

post-war the term 'friend' is used. In this phase they represent Mottram's most significant contact – war experience links the two men.

Unlike Skene, however, Dormer seems unalienated from England. At the end of *The Crime at Vanderlynden's* he looks at the 'moderately white cliffs of England' and, beyond them, for him 'lay his occupation and his home, his true mental environment, and native aspiration' (p. 786). These are the things he is escaping to, and Mottram does not seem to be asking for an ironic response, even though the relevant stories in *Ten Years Ago* can be read as providing an ironic dimension. Not long before the passage just quoted, Mottram has stressed that Dormer has not been assimilated to France: 'Dormer remained a stranger in France . . . he was difficult to assimilate . . . (p. 783). Dormer, then, remains rooted in his Englishness, and Dormer is a modestly optimistic man.

At one point in his war service, Dormer sees a headless corpse and this headless man enters his consciousness, to trouble his rest. He associates it with the private soldiers and also with the unknown soldier who had damaged the shrine at the farm. As Dormer looks towards England he contemplates the rankers also waiting to return and he admires their 'lugubrious humour'. He reflects that 'no disaster and no triumph could alter their island characteristics, however much talk there might be about town life sapping the race (p. 784). Dormer is not a ranker, but the passage from which I have been quoting merges these common soldiers with the provincial officer. Parallel to the unchanging nature of the Flemish peasant Madeleine Vanderlynden there is the racial permanence of these men, men who are seen as having 'island characteristics' and who are essentially unaffected by urbanization.

Mottram would seem to be gesturing to the enduring myth of an harmonious rural England. It is the permanence of these English which allows Mottram to avoid the disturbing thought of revolution, but it is avoided at some cost.

In the first place the emphasis on Englishness represents retreat from any idea of internationalism, and is therefore the logical product of that failure of contact which has run through the trilogy. England, it seems, will escape disaster, as Flanders will by remaining separate. By implication the cost will involve fighting again across historic landscapes in the future. But Mottram can offer optimism also only by providing for Dormer a distinctly external view of the private soldiers. He sees them as 'herded and stalled like animals, but cheerful in their queer way'. Their minds 'were as drab as their uniform, so inarticulate, so decent and likable in their humility and good temper. Theirs was the true Republicanism . . .' (p. 784). As the war ends there is protest from the men, chiefly about demobilization,[1] and Mottram's officers are understanding: 'It's too bad, hangin' 'em up for months and months, while other people get their jobs . . . think of what the men have done' (p. 780). Because of the 'decency' of the men 'The Headless Man was fading out' of Dormer's consciousness.

A striking feature of these closing pages is the sense of separateness. Dormer does not see himself as identified with the privates, and the officers who sympathize with the men's demands see the latter's problems as exclusively theirs alone. These officers show no sense that they, themselves, might face similar problems. It would be easy to see these pages as simply condescending, marking an unwillingness or inability to understand the private soldiers except in terms of the mass and to characterize them in collective terms which stress humility and cheerful endurance. But the matter is not so simple. It has to be admitted, I think, that Dormer's view has a certain validity, for the history of the British 'masses' does include a great deal of endurance, some of it cheerful, and a slowness to push protest to extremes. The disappointments of the years immediately after the war and the miserable unemployment of the 1920s and 1930s did lead to protest, some of it violent, but there was no revolution. It should be added that this does not prove anything about irreducible features of those seen as constituting the British masses, but it does suggest that the structures of British society have managed to keep many people 'herded and stalled like animals', encouraging cheerfulness as a way of avoiding revolution. Dormer's 'essential Englishness', then, can be seen as a generalization from the position of a dominant class, and its strength lies in its complacent description of social characteristics as inherent features of the mass. Minds need not be drab, nor mouths inarticulate. If and when the masses have bright minds and articulate voices, there may be for the Dormers less decency, less 'humility and good temper'. That truth has been known in Britain for centuries. Yet it remains true that Dormer's vision is closer to the truth of Britain's experience since 1918 than either Barbusse's socialist vision or Romains' land of bandits. Mottram, it seems, can tolerate the deracinations he charts because, whether in Flanders or Britain, there is a rootedness which is durable, racist and conservative. Howard's End endures; Leonard Bast must die.

Like Mottram, Ford Madox Ford produced three volumes centred on the war, which may be treated as a trilogy. In Ford's case, however, there is the complication of a fourth novel, *The Last Post,* which continues the story beyond the war's end. Although it can be argued that Ford has produced a tetralogy rather than a trilogy, I shall treat *The Last Post* as a pendant to the other three volumes.[2]

Mottram, as we have seen, varies his centres of consciousness while using the Spanish Farm as his focus. By contrast Ford's trilogy has a dominant central consciousness, that of Christopher Tietjens, one which is so marked that the material is largely, though not entirely, mediated through his mind. The external time-span, which extends from just before the outbreak of war to just after the end, is interwoven with the infolded, simultaneous patterns of time in Tietjens' mind to create a complex double time-scale which allows Ford to associate materials which are separate in terms of serial chronology. There is a parallel to this in Ford's presentation of ideas of rootedness, for although much of this is internal in *Parade's End* (what characters believe in, are committed to or obsessed by) it has its external complement in the house of the Tietjens family (Groby) and in the Duchemin home which is the setting for the breakfast scene in *Some Do Not . . .* (part I, chapter 5).

Christopher Tietjens himself is presented as having a strong sense of his roots. He is 'the youngest son of a Yorkshire country gentleman' (*Some Do Not . . .*, p. 13) and a Tory. He is known as brilliant yet of independent mind, and is highly conscious of class and race. Tietjens sees himself as essentially of the eighteenth century, but there are also intimated links with Christ, which are particularly strong in the final volume. Ford further suggests that Tietjens is scruffy and physically rather odd. These elements carry two main sugges-tions. They indicate Tietjens' social and cultural roots and they clearly associate him with power and privilege. Groby is the main indication that the Tietjens' connection with power and privilege is carried by the country house tradition, the land/power link being, of course, set deep in English history. Nevertheless, it is clear that Ford does not wish us to see Tietjens as, in any simple way, a type of English country gentleman. There is his brilliance, which brings respect, but also some suspicion. There is his appearance (e.g. 'He came, grey all over . . . and lopsided', *A Man Could Stand Up,* p. 159). And there are the suggested links with Christ (thus Valentine thinks of him as 'saintly; Godlike, Jesus-Christ-like', *A Man Could Stand Up,* p. 33, and his first name incorporates 'Christ'). These features give Tietjens a separateness in his class, which is increased by the fact that Groby has a north of England Catholic, or recusant, context. Christopher Tietjens is Anglican, but his wife is Catholic and both Christopher and his elder brother, Mark, are deeply conscious of their Catholic background. The separateness of Christopher Tietjens shades into the idea that he is an anachronism: 'I'm a Tory of such an extinct type that she might take me for anything. The last megatherium . . .' (*No More Parades,* p. 180).

Talented and privileged though Tietjens is, however, he is not a social or professional success. At the beginning of the trilogy he is a relatively minor official in 'the newly created Imperial Department of Statistics under Sir Reginald Ingleby' (*Some Do Not . . .,* p. 11) and, although Tietjens' statistical abilities are thought highly of, it is the low-born Scot, Macmaster, who becomes powerful, influential and rewarded, while Tietjens is on the brink of losing his job. Nor is Tietjens a success in the army. He ends the war still only a major and has had considerable trouble with higher authority. His failure is marked in other ways too. His marriage has broken when the first volume begins and, however impossible Sylvia may be, the fact of a failed marriage is seen as a social failure. By the end of the third volume Groby is in the hands of Sylvia and General Campion (in *The Last Post* the loosening of the Tietjens connection with the house is taken further, as Sylvia plans to let it to Americans). Even at this stage Tietjens has not consummated his relationship with Valentine Wannop, a relationship which is central to all three volumes, and he has suffered shell-shock.

We have seen that Gilbert Frankau ended his novel *Peter Jackson, Cigar Merchant* with the harmony of the dance in celebration of the Armistice, thereby claiming that the war had changed nothing very much. Frankau can suggest that what matters, what is rooted, endures and that the damage which the war has brought to combatants can be healed by love and Baynet. Ford concludes his third volume, *A Man Could Stand Up*, with what might be seen as a version of this. The Armistice is being celebrated and Tietjens is in company in his apartment at the centre of London. But what Ford creates is a grotesque carnival rather than an harmonious dance:

> They were prancing. The whole world round them was yelling and prancing round. They were the centre of unending roaring circles. The man with the eyeglass had stuck a half-crown in his other eye. He was well-meaning. A brother ... She was frightened. She was amazed. Did you ever! He was swaying slowly. The elephant! ... A dear, meal-sack elephant. She was setting out on ... (pp. 188–9)

Clearly, Ford's carnival of the injured and the drunk is his view of the world at the end of the vast effort and strain which the war had been, but it also suggests where Tietjens now is. The lines just quoted present the impressions of Valentine Wannop, who sees Tietjens as an elephant, and the dots which end the novel represent the uncertainty of their future, if they have one together. The elephant image has a strong anachronistic element: what function does an elephant have in a modern industrialized nation, except as zoo-exhibit or circus performer? This raises questions about Tietjens' future in relation to his immediate past, in the war, and to what he represents about the more distant past, of Groby and what it has stood for. The location of the last moments of *A Man Could Stand Up* is not Groby but Tietjens' London apartment, but this is an empty place, the furniture largely removed and the wife gone.

Tietjens is, in some important respects, much like other protagonists of novels about the Great War. His relations with Staff and home have not been good, and his sympathies associate him with those who share life at the front rather than with those who are running the war at a distance. He concerns himself with the conditions of the men under him and is sensitive to the strains of the line. Consequently the Tietjens of the front sequences is neurotic, jumpy and anxious over the failure of his memory:

> It might of course be the signal for the German barrage to begin. Tietjens' heart stopped; his skin on the nape of the neck began to prickle; his hands were cold. That was fear: the BATTLE FEAR, experienced in *strafes*. He might not again be able to hear himself think. Not ever. What did he want of life? . . . Well, just not to lose his reason . . . (*A Man Could Stand Up,* p. 83)

At the end of the trilogy, although Tietjens is in a group of sorts he is not really of it:

They were all yelling.

'Good old Tietjens! Good old Fat Man! Pre-war Hooch! He'd be the one to get it.' No one like Fat Man Tietjens! He lounged at the door; easy, benevolent. In uniform now. (p. 188)

Although Tietjens is the focus here there is no sense at the end of *A Man Could Stand Up* that he is the leader of some new formation. Neither a joiner nor actively political before the war, there is nothing to suggest that these negatives have been made positive by his war experiences. When Ford came to write *The Last Post* he made no effort to alter this aspect of Tietjens, who is a revenant in that pendant novel.

Post-war is not much of a consideration in Ford's trilogy, but the image of the elephant which was touched on above, together with the material facts of Tietjens' condition at the war's end, is enough to suggest that he is displaced. What, it seems, he carries forward from the war is a developed sense of alienation, a damaged memory and an empty purse. There is nothing to hint either that he has a redefined view of a role for himself in post-war society or any sense that the war has anything positive to offer post-war. All that Tietjens plans is a relationship with Valentine Wannop and a connected career in antiques.

It would not be wholly accurate to suggest that the war has uprooted Christopher Tietjens. The failure of his marriage, the doubts about the paternity of his son and heir, together with the first encounter with Valentine, are the immediate causes of the shaking loose of Ford's protagonist: in a sense, the war is only the confirmation of the social mess which Tietjens is in. But the war does take further Tietjens' alienation from his natural society, while failing to provide him with any compensation. Tietjens is capable of seeing further than most into the opinions and beliefs of others (notably of those who oppose the war), and he is also capable of strong feelings for the needs and wants of men serving under him, but he does not find any new group or groups to compensate for the heightened alienation he feels from society at home. Tietjens is clear that he wants Valentine, but the war frustrates the chances of consummation and produces such distancing that he almost, at times, forgets what he does want. And, of course, Tietjens' role in the war itself has hardly been glorious, having more to do with requisitions and the dispatch of troops than with gallant hand-to-hand combat or rescuing a friend in No Man's Land.

Elephants are perhaps irrelevant in twentieth-century Britain. In his Sherston 'memoirs' Siegfried Sassoon had organized his material to suggest that the war broke up an Edwardian idyll, while Blunden's harmless shepherd pose carries similar implications. Ford does not suggest that the war made an elephant of Christopher Tietjens: his anachronism is discernible before the war and the war confirms it. In that sense the war belongs to a process rather than creating a new one, and Tietjens is doomed to live as a reminder of the past, his occupation as an antiques dealer being appropriate enough.

What then are we to make of what this elephant stands for? We have noted that Tietjens is sometimes seen, within the novels, as Christ-like, and we saw in chapter 1 that there were other novelists who introduced ideas of Christ into their views of the war. In so far as Tietjens is both a Christ and an anachronism the configuration is a disturbing one. If we see Tietjens as serving others humbly in the war, and remember that there seems to be little function for him post-war, the suggestion would seem to be that there is little room for Christs any more. If we add that, in the context of the war, Tietjens-as-Christ is admired but seen as rather a nuisance there is also the suggestion that the war has little time either for Tietjens' code or Christ's.

It was mentionead earlier that, in *The Last Post*, Ford has Sylvia Tietjens contemplating letting Groby to Americans. There is also the matter of cutting down the great tree which is part of the house's setting and of local legend about Groby and the Tietjens family. Christopher Tietjens is not the natural heir of Groby – that role has fallen to his brother Mark, and Mark comes into his inheritance on the death of his father, who is killed when his gun goes off, either by accident or suicide (a matter which is left unresolved). But Mark Tietjens does not want Groby. In *The Last Post* Mark, who has had a fit at the Armistice terms, lies waiting for his death in the garden of a small house, where he has retired with his long-term French mistress (now wife). Groby is no part of the last days of Mark Tietjens. Christopher Tietjens' attitude to the house is more complex, but the essential point is that he does not become its master. Nor is there any assurance of a Tietjens future, since Mark has no children and Christopher's son may not even be his child.

The cutting down of the great tree of Groby is thus obvious in its symbolism, and with reference to Christopher himself it would seem to indicate that what he stands for has no part to play in the post-war world. It is important here to remember that, in the trilogy, Tietjens has been seen as largely isolated. At the opening of *Some Do Not . . .* he is with Macmaster, but the relationship is very carefully presented as having marked limits, and what closeness there is passes as the trilogy proceeds. Tietjens has no real friends; his marriage has been a disaster; he has little to do with his own family; and he makes no close relationships in the war with fellow officers, let alone with any ranker. The exception is obviously Valentine Wannop, and we are clearly meant to see Christopher and Valentine as belonging to each other, but the fact remains that, at the trilogy's end, they have still to make love, let alone live together.

Tietjens is, then, perforce an independent figure, and intellectual independence is one of his attributes. This allows him to see beyond the surface, to escape various cants, and it is also, of course, this which makes him valued, respected, but also suspected and held at a distance, in the public and social world to which he belongs by birth and class. But Tietjens, largely independent of that world, does not find another. Although he can see some way into the pacifism associated with Valentine (and more strongly with her brother) he never comes close to being one of those who resisted the war. He is suspected of being a socialist, but is never anywhere near to that. Neither, however, does he develop along the lines of Lawrence's Richard Somers: he shows no sign of moving towards that sort of extreme right-wing attitude. As we have seen, he belongs to a tradition which can be associated with the country house, but Groby has passed from the Tietjens and its tree is to fall. Tietjens is finally an elephant.

The war did not, Ford's trilogy suggests, cause all this. It is part of a process anterior to its outbreak, and this is a sound historical view. But the war has done nothing to hinder the process and it has not led Tietjens to any position from which he might see a way of opposing it in socio-political terms. Survival as the antique-dealing lover of Valentine Wannop is the most there is for him, and there is nothing in *The Last Post* to alter this analysis. Elephants are not dinosaurs, but they are certainly not electric trains. Consideration of Ford's life and works, such as that provided by Mizener, would suggest that Ford must have regretted the suggested passing of the world of Groby. It is to Ford's creative credit that in *Parade's End* he offers an account of a passing which is much more than nostalgic. Tietjens has complex integrity and he is presented with considerable roundness. This allows a reader to go beyond the feeling that there is no public future for this Tory gentleman. Ford creates a sense of historical process which is sufficiently intricate to allow speculation as to whether such figures as Tietjens had ever operated efficaciously in anything but the worlds of Tory mythology, wherein, of course, they still have a shadowy being. If, after the war, there are any roots they are not for Christopher Tietjens.

Conclusion

It is not surprising that the Great War has given rise
to a vast literature of many kinds and in many lan-
guages. This literature begins with the war's beginning, continues throughout the war, and is still being
written. No earlier war, so far as I know, gave rise to
an equivalent body of writing and, for the first time, at
least so far as the British were concerned, there was
the possibility of a substantial literature produced by
combatants, for the armies of the Great War were the
first literate British armies.

Fiction forms only one part of this output, and,
almost by definition, fiction of this war could represent
only certain angles of vision. The basic level of literacy
among the rankers could scarcely lead to sustained
narratives of the kind expected of the novel (although
oral narrative is another matter), while many officers
were hardly better equipped for such demands.
Moreover, it is obvious that both combatants with pre-
war experience of writing fiction and those who learnt
to write out of war experience could scarcely compose
novels at the front, which is one reason why so much
of the significant fiction of the war appears only some
years after its end. By definition, non-combatants
were in a better position to produce fiction dealing
with the war while it was still going on, but even these

writers had the difficult problem of assimilation to cope with.

The fiction which was the product of the war is very various and its heterogeneity makes a coherent view difficult to achieve. Large parts of the total output have been mainly ignored in this book. Much more, for example, might have been written about memoir-as-fiction and there is room for a book about 'popular' novels of the war. Frankau's *Peter Jackson* and Raymond's *Tell England* have both been discussed here, while another good example is John Oxenham's *1914* (Methuen, 1916). Oxenham's novel is a compendium of stock attitudes and myths. It uses the stereotypes of the heroic young male and the pure and loyal young female, sending these on a journey to and from Germany just before the war and during its opening months. The account of the journey is shaped both to define the moral quality of the young English couple and to establish Germany's isolation as a bestial nation. Oxenham also, significantly, sees England as both rural and middle-class.

There are a number of novels about the war which were written by women, and these also have been largely ignored here. Vera Brittain's *Honourable Estate* (Gollancz, 1936) and Rose Macaulay's *Non-Combatants and Others* (Hodder and Stoughton, 1916) have more to say about unease over the war than most male novels, but I do not feel sure of my grasp of either book. A woman should, however, make a study of these and other war novels by women.

I am not unduly concerned to rank the novels I have discussed either within the category of war fiction or in the history of the English novel. Most of them have obvious enough defects and there are several which seem to me to be meretricious – *Mr Standfast* and *Tell*

[136]

England come most readily to mind. The war's challenge made the writing of formally coherent and controlled novels very difficult, so that it can be argued that some of the best fiction rooted in the war is not directly about it to any great extent. Graham Greene's *It's a Battlefield,* for example, uses the language of the war to define post-war England and Lawrence's *Women in Love* depends in many ways upon the experience of the war. A less well-known case is that of Grassic Gibbon's *Scots Quair.* Gibbon writes about a Scotland far distant from the social and cultural worlds of most fiction of the war, and it is this which gives his trilogy its particular significance as, among other things, an account of how the war affected regions far away from the front. In this sense Gibbon is concerned with the theme of roots and uprootings which is considered in the last chapter of the present book.

The value of the novels I have discussed, however, lies less in their formal properties than in what they manage to say, sometimes perhaps unconsciously, about the war. It can be argued that the shrill obsessions of *Kangaroo* and the distorting anger of *Death of a Hero,* while being formal defects, are extremely revealing as responses to the war's pressures. Ford's trilogy is perhaps the richest fiction to come from the war, with the mind of Christopher Tietjens drawing together a remarkable diversity of material; but Ford's achievement should not blind us to Bensted's honesty nor make us miss how revealing are the limits of Mottram's social vision. The novels may be most revealing when they are most objectionable, as with Buchan's crudeness and Wells's inadequate ironic liberalism. These novels come into their own, I think, not when viewed purely aesthetically

[137]

(which would be obscene) but when read as products of,
and contributions to history, in the broad and proper
sense of that word.

Notes

Introduction

1 There is a convenient symposium on *The Outbreak of the First World War,* ed. D. Lee, Heath, 1963.

Chapter I: Some Patterns

1 The *DNB* tells us that Buchan knew *Pilgrim's Progress* 'almost by heart', but Mary seems to credit Richard with a prodigious capacity for fast memorizing.

2 John Laffin (ed. *Letters from the Front,* Dent, 1973, p. 15) refers to A. D. Gillespie, killed at Loos, whose body was apparently found with a marked text of Bunyan's book on it.

3 Behind Hannay, if rather shadowily, are Nietzsche's ideas of the superior, 'aristocratic' man, with a contempt for the masses, a strong will to power and the view that only the strong should survive.

4 Both critiques are reproduced in the Sphere edition, 1968, Preface. The edition from which I quote is the first (Bles, 1930).

5 Some of 'Sapper's' stories purport, quite unconvincingly, to represent the ranker-perspective, while John Harris's *Covenant with Death* is a ranker novel written a long time after the war (Hutchinson, 1961). The major ranker novels, however, tend to be American and German.

6 Both cited in the Preface mentioned in note 4 above. For *Tarka* etc., see the biographical note on Williamson.

7 See Paul Fussell, *The Great War and Modern Memory*
(1975), Oxford, 1979, pp. 117–18. The identification of
soldier with Christ and the crucifixion is also illustrated
by Mark Girouard, *The Return to Camelot,* Yale, 1981,
esp. p. 275ff.

8 First published anonymously and in a limited edition, in
1929, with the title *The Middle Parts of Fortune.*
Republished, expurgated, in 1930, as *Her Privates We* (by
'Private 19022'). First full public text, with ascription to
Manning, by Peter Davies in 1977.

9 Both Manning's Bourne and Aldington's Winterbourne
(see chapter 2) may remind readers of Hamlet's definition
of death as 'The undiscovered country, from whose
bourn/No traveller returns' (III. i. 79–80). The names
seem appropriate, since both soldiers die and both are
'travellers' to and through war to death. Aldington's
'Winter–' strengthens the negative connotations of the
name.

10 For the Hague Peace Conference and for the defining of
equipment see Barbara Tuchman, *The Proud Tower,*
Macmillan, 1966, p. 277 ff.

11 For comment on a later and more overt criticism of sport
imagery see Extended Notes, p. 142.

Chapter II: Richard Aldington and Transformation

1 Such problems were not unique to Aldington and are
clearly related to the repression discussed by Eric Leed in
No Man's Land, Cambridge, 1979. See his chapter 5 and
particularly pp. 190–2.

2 Such experiments with form link Aldington with certain
Modernists: he is following in the wake of such as Proust
and Eliot.

3 Similar points about style could be made with reference to
Modernism at large. Wyndham Lewis comments that
Aldington was one of the signatories of the 'major
Manifesto (of the "Great London Vortex")' (*Blasting and
Bombardiering,* 1937; revised edition 1967; Calder, 1982,
p. 37).

4 This style owes much to Lewis, again associating Aldington with aspects of Modernism.

Chapter III: The Return of the Soldier

1 See John Lucas, *Modern English Poetry*, Batsford, 1986, and M. J. Wiener, *English Culture and the Decline of the Industrial Spirit, 1850–1980* (1981), Penguin, 1985.

Chapter IV: The Novelist at Home

1 On the Little Mother see Fussell pp. 216–18; on 'gross dichotomizing' see Leed *passim.*
2 Britling's name suggests that he speaks, in some sense, for Britain, but the novel is very much *English*, its country-house myth and associated values having little to do with the rest of Britain.
3 See Raymond Williams, *The English Novel from Dickens to Lawrence,* Chatto and Windus, 1976.
4 Lawrence, however, reverses this account in 'England, My England'.
5 On this see David Boulton, *Objection Overruled,* MacGibbon and Kee, 1967.

Chapter V: Roots and Uprootings

1 See D. Lamb, *Mutinies: 1917–20,* Solidarity, n.d.; A. Rothstein, *The Soldiers' Strikes of 1919,* Macmillan, 1980; G. Dallas and D. Gill, *The Unknown Army,* Verso, 1985.
2 *Some Do Not . . .* (1924), *No More Parades* (1925), *A Man Could Stand Up* (1926). The volumes are presented as a trilogy in the Bodley Head Ford of 1963. My references are to the Sphere edition of 1969.

Extended Notes

Novels and Memoirs

Richard Aldington claims that *Death of a Hero* is not
really a novel (see p. 47). But one of the most
interesting aspects of the question 'When is a novel not
a novel?' concerns the relationship between the novel
and the memoir. Novelists of the war often present
their fictions as accounts of individual lives (so Forester, Aldington, Manning) and this is, of course, in line
with a major tradition of the English novel. But several
writers who deal with the Great War purport to be
providing memoir rather than fiction, yet clearly leave
room for doubt. The blurring between fiction and
memoir occurs famously with Siegfried Sassoon, who
writes the 'memoirs' of George Sherston and also his
own. Sherston is clearly not Sassoon, but the overlap is
considerable and both sets of memoirs can be seen as
versions of one body of material. In chapter 5 of *The
Weald of Youth* (1942) Sassoon seems to want Sherston
to be both himself and a fiction. Moreover, Sassoon's
war diaries make it clear that 'fictionalization' is not
confined to the relationship between Sherston and
Sassoon, for the relatively raw material of the diaries
has been imaginatively shaped to create the memoirs of
Sassoon, whereby it can be argued that 'Sassoon' is as

much a fictional character as 'Sherston'. In *Three Personal Records of the War* (Scholartis, 1929) two of the authors, Easton and Partridge, use the same device as Sassoon does in the Sherston memoirs. Other examples of blurring are obvious enough. Robert Graves, in *Goodbye to All That,* uses material which is not autobiographical in any usual sense, while Edmund Blunden's *Undertones of War* is artfully shaped into a kind of bio-fiction about a harmless young shepherd in the tradition of literary pastoral. Wyndham Lewis's *Blasting and Bombardiering* avoids the issue by confronting it head-on in the very first paragraph: 'And a good biography is of course a sort of novel.' Paul Fussell discusses fiction as memoir in his *The Great War and Modern Memory* (see especially chapters 3, 5).

War and sport: a late version

The most explicit hostile commentary on the 'cavalry and cricket' mentality which I have come across is in John Harris's 1961 novel, *Covenant With Death.* Early in the novel, which concentrates on ranker experience, Mark Fenner, when enlisting, is spoken to by Earl FitzJames, who asks him 'Play any games?' Fenner says he does and FitzJames comments 'That's the stuff . . . Sporting spirit. Don't hit a man when he's down. Yer in for the greatest game of yer life, young feller.' Such a view is attacked later when Fenner tells the NCO, Bold, that he is refusing a stripe, and Bold comments:

> You want to *play* at being soldiers all the time . . . You want to fight the Germans fairly. No kicking. No gouging. No going behind their backs. No fouls and no offside. A great big beautiful game of cricket. Well played, chaps! Jolly good show! Scrag the Hun, fellows, and hurrah for General 'Aig.

To the professional soldier Bold, Fenner is an amateur, his attitudes those of the officer-gentleman (even though Fenner is neither). Later again, Bold is addressed by a young officer after a futile and bloody fight: 'Were you with us, or in front?' Bold replies 'Second and first waves ... This is all that's left,' and Harris continues:

> 'Well played, chaps,' the officer said, 'you're a bloody fine lot – ' His voice trailed off unsteadily and he looked around him, his eyes staring.
>
> 'I've got nobody – ' He paused and gulped, looking like a lost child. 'I've lost all my chaps. Every bloody one of them. They're all out there.'

Some pages on survivors moving back pass 'hundreds of fresh soldiers moving up, men who were clean and unstained with blood'. Fenner 'felt them patting (him) on the back'. Someone says 'Well played, chaps' and an incoming officer asks Fenner 'What was it like?' Fenner replies 'Like a butcher's shop.' He is then asked if many officers were lost and answers 'We lost the lot' and reflects on how he 'somehow drew an immense bitter satisfaction from the shocked look on his clean, well-shaven face'. (The quotations come from pp. 22, 201, 344–5, 371–2.) By way of contrast, in addition to material discussed in chapter I, there are events like that of a company of the East Surreys going over the top dribbling a football and the use of sporting imagery by poets like Henley and Newbolt before the war. The most famous of such poems is Newbolt's 'Vitaï Lampada'.

Biographical Notes

(These notes are restricted to novelists whose work is discussed at some length in the text.)

Aldington, E. G. (Richard) (1892–1962) Born Portsmouth. Father a solicitor's clerk. Educated Dover College and University College, London. Volunteered in 1914 but service delayed on medical grounds until 1916. Originally a private in the Royal Sussex Regiment, later lieutenant and acting captain. Known as a poet before the war and married the poet H[ilda] D[oolittle]. Critic, translator, film writer, author of seven novels. Left England in 1928.

Bennett, E. A. (Arnold) (1867–1931) Born Hanley, Staffs. Father a solicitor (former potter and teacher); mother the daughter of a Derbyshire weaver. Of a non-conformist family, Bennett was educated at Burslem Endowed School and the Newcastle-under-Lyme Middle School. Entered father's office in 1885 and a London firm of solicitors as clerk in 1888. Journalist, prolific novelist, playwright. Lived in France 1902–12 and was too old for active service.

Bensted, C. R. (1896–1980) Born Cambridge. Educated Cambridge and County High School and Cambridge University. Subaltern in the Royal Artillery from 1915, won the MC and returned to Cambridge in 1919. A county cricketer, he joined the Royal Navy after university and retired in 1946 as Instructor-Captain. Apart from

*Retreat,*Bensted wrote about the sea, Cambridge and the legislature, as well as translating two books from the French. (I owe this information to Canon Alan Wilkinson, who referred me to Dr S. C. Aston's obituary notice for Bensted in the St Catharine's College Society Magazine.)

Buchan, John (First Baron Tweedsmuir) (1875–1940) Born Perth, of a Border Lowland family. Father a Free Church of Scotland minister; mother a farmer's daughter. Educated Hutcheson Boys Grammar School and the Universities of Glasgow and Oxford. Was in South Africa with Lord Milner 1901–3 and joined Nelson's (publishers) in 1907. On the staff of *The Times* at the front in 1915, became a major in the Intelligence Corps (1916) and, later, Subordinate Director at the Department of Information. M.P. (Conservative) for the Scottish Universities 1927–35. Governor-General of Canada 1935. Author of a number of novels and a twenty-four-volume *History of the Great War*.

Ford, Ford Madox (Ford Hermann Hueffer) (1873–1939) Born Merton, Surrey. Father a German music critic; mother a daughter of the painter Ford Madox Brown. Educated privately at a school in Folkstone and at University College School, London. An established poet, essayist and novelist before the war. Collaborated with Conrad and founded the *English Review*. Commissioned in the Royal Welch Fusiliers (1915), saw active service and was gassed. Died in France.

Forester, C. S. (1899–1966) Born in Cairo, grew up in London. Educated at Dulwich College and Guy's Hospital. Explorer and journalist (with experience in Spain and Czechoslovakia), his first novel was published in 1926 and he had fourteen books to his name before *The General*.

Frankau, Gilbert (1884–1952) Born London. Father a wholesale cigar merchant; mother a novelist. Educated at Eton, leaving to join cigar business. Joined up in 1914; was commissioned in the East Surrey Regiment, but transferred to the Royal Field Artillery; served at Ypres, Loos, the Somme; invalided out in 1918 with shell-shock. Poet and novelist. Became politically of the extreme right.

Lawrence, D. H. (1885–1930) Born Eastwood, Notts. Son of a miner. Educated Nottingham High School, which he left to work in surgical goods, before becoming a pupil teacher. Qualified as a teacher at Nottingham University College. Had first novel published in 1911 and lived by his writing thereafter (except for a short period teaching). Married Frieda von Richthofen in 1914; left England in 1919 and travelled/lived on the Continent, Australia and America, until dying of tuberculosis.

Manning, Frederic (1887–1935) Born Sydney, Australia. Attended Sydney Grammar School but mainly self-educated. Despite asthma he served in the ranks in Flanders, Artois and Picardy. Lived in Italy after the war. Poet, author of one novel and a biography.

Mottram, R. H. (1883–1971) Born Norwich. Father a bank clerk; mother a teacher. Joined father's bank; became a junior officer in 1914 and served through the war. Gave up banking for writing in 1927. *The Spanish Farm* (filmed as *Roses in Picardy*) was the first of his many novels.

Raymond, Ernest (1888–1974) Educated at St Paul's School and Chichester Theological College. Served as a chaplain during the war but thereafter had a crisis of faith and resigned from Orders. Author of some 40 novels.

Wells, H. G. (1866–1946) Born Bromley, Kent. Father in turn a gardener, a professional cricketer and a shopkeeper; mother daughter of a Sussex innkeeper. Wells was largely self-taught, a student teacher at fourteen, before working for a chemist and a draper. After teaching again, he attended the Normal School of Science (under T. H.

Huxley) and became a Fabian. More teaching, in Wrexham
and Kilburn; B.Sc (London) 1890; tutor at University
Tutorial College, London, 1891; Labour parliamentary
candidate for London University 1922, 1923.

West, Rebecca (Cicely Isabel Fairfield) (1892–1983) Born Co.
Kerry. Father an army officer and war correspondent;
mother a musician. Educated at George Watson's Ladies
College, Edinburgh, and drama school. Briefly an actress,
then a journalist, and active before the war in the suffrage
movement. Married a banker in 1930, having given birth
to Anthony West, by H. G. Wells, in 1914. Essayist,
novelist and travel writer.

Williamson, Henry (1897–1977) Born Bedfordshire. Privately
educated. Enlisted as a private at seventeen, served
through the war and returned home in poor mental
condition. Lived rough until first novel stabilized him.
Tarka the Otter (1927 Hawthornden Prize) established
him, and he settled to writing and farming in Norfolk.
Became politically of the extreme right. Novelist and
nature writer, he published a sequence of novels centred
on the war.

Bibliography

(Apart from the books used in the text I have included here other works which a reader may find of help and interest.)

English novels and short stories

Aldington, Richard, *All Men are Enemies,* Chatto and Windus, 1933
Death of a Hero (1929), Consul, 1965
Roads to Glory, Chatto and Windus, 1930
Soft Answers, Chatto and Windus, 1932
The Colonel's Daughter, Chatto and Windus, 1931

Bagnold, Enid, *The Happy Foreigner,* William Heinemann, 1920

Bennett, Arnold, *The Roll-Call,* Hutchinson & Co., 1918
The Pretty Lady (1918), Cassell, 1932
Lord Raingo, Cassell, 1926

Bensted, C. R., *Retreat,* Methuen & Co., 1930

Brittain, Vera, *Honourable Estate,* Victor Gollancz, 1936

Bruce, George (ed.), *Short Stories of the First World War,* Sidgwick and Jackson, 1971

Buchan, John, *Greenmantle* (1916), Penguin Books, 1956
Mr Standfast (1919), Pan Books, 1964

Conrad, Joseph, 'The Tale' (1925), in *Tales of Hearsay,* J. M. Dent & Sons, 1955

Dawson, A. J., *Somme Battle Stories,* Hodder and Stoughton, 1916

[149]

Dunsany, Lord, *Tales of War*, Fisher Unwin, 1918
Ewart, Wilfred, *Way of Revelation*, Putnam & Co., 1921
Ford, Ford Madox, *Parade's End:*
>>> – *Some Do Not . . .* (1924), Sphere Books, 1969
>>> – *No More Parades* (1925), Sphere Books, 1969
>>> – *A Man Could Stand Up* (1926), Sphere Books, 1969
>>> *The Last Post,* Gerald Duckworth & Co., 1928
Forester, C. S., *The General* (1936), Penguin Books, 1979
Frankau, Gilbert, *Peter Jackson, Cigar Merchant,* Hutchinson & Co., 1920
>>> *Three Englishmen,* Hutchinson & Co., n.d.
Harris, John, *Covenant with Death* (1961), Companion Book Club, 1962
'Hay, Ian', *The First Hundred Thousand,* W. Blackwood & Sons Ltd, 1916
>>> *Carrying On – After the First Hundred Thousand,* W. Blackwood & Sons Ltd, 1917
Isherwood, Christopher, *The Memorial,* Hogarth Press, 1931
Kipling, Rudyard, 'The Brushwood Boy', in *The Day's Work* (1898), Macmillan, 1964
>>> 'Mary Postgate', in *A Choice of Kipling's Prose*, Faber and Faber, 1987
Lawrence, D. H., *Kangaroo* (1932), Penguin Books, 1950
Macaulay, Rose, *Non-Combatants and Others,* Hodder and Stoughton, 1916
M'Fee, William, *Command,* Secker and Warburg, 1922
Manning, Frederic, *Her Privates We* (1929), Peter Davies Ltd, 1977
Morris, W. F., *Bretherton, in Four Dramatic War Novels,* Odhams, n.d.
Mottram, R. H., *The Spanish Farm Trilogy:*
>>> – *The Spanish Farm* (1924), Chatto and Windus, 1927

     — *Sixty-Four, Ninety-Four* (1925), Chatto
  and Windus, 1927

     — *The Crime at Vanderlynden's* (1926),
  Chatto and Windus, 1927

  Ten Years Ago, Chatto and Windus, 1928

Oxenham, John, *1914*, Methuen & Co., 1916

Raymond, Ernest, *Tell England,* Cassell, 1922

'Sapper', *Men, Women and Guns,* Hodder and Stoughton, 1916

Strang, Herbert, *Fighting with French,* Frowde, 1915

Wells, H. G., *Joan and Peter,* Waterlow Publishers Ltd, 1933
         Mr Britling Sees It Through, Waterlow
         Publishers Ltd, 1933

West, Rebecca, *The Return of the Soldier* (1918), in *A
  Celebration,* Penguin Books, 1978

Williamson, Henry, *The Patriot's Progress,* Bles, 1930

Yeates, V. M., *Winged Victory* (1934), Mayflower Books, 1974

Other novels

Barbusse, Henri, *Le Feu* (1916); translated as *Under Fire* by
  W. Fitzwater Wray (1917), J. M. Dent & Sons, 1965

Boyd, Thomas, *Through the Wheat,* Scribner's, 1923

Cather, Willa, *One of Ours* (1922), Hamish Hamilton, 1965

cummings, e.e., *The Enormous Room* (1922), Granada
  Publishing, 1978

Dos Passos, John, *One Man's Initiation* (1917), Cornell
  University Press, 1969

Faulkner, William, *Soldiers' Pay* (1926), Liveright Publishing
  Corp., 1970

Hemingway, Ernest, *A Farewell to Arms* (1929), Penguin
  Books, 1935

Hasek, Jaroslav, *The Good Soldier Svejk* (1922), translated
  by C. Parrott, Penguin Books, 1974

Jünger, Ernst, *In Stahlgewittern* (1920); translated as *Storm
of Steel* by B. Creighton, Chatto and Windus, 1929

Remarque, Ernst, *Im Westen Nichts Neues* (1929); translated
         as *All Quiet on the Western Front* by A. W.
         Wheen, Putnam & Co., 1929

> Der Weg zurück (1931); translated as The
> Road Back by A. W. Wheen, Mayflower
> Books, 1979

Romains, Jules, Verdun (1938); translated with same title by
    G. Hopkins (1939), Mayflower Books, 1973

Wharton, Edith, A Son at the Front, Scribner's, 1923

Zweig, Arnold, Der Streit um den Sergeanten Grischa (1927);
    translated as The Case of Sergeant Grischa by E. Sutton,
    Secker and Warburg, 1928

Autobiography, biography, memoir, diary

Aldington, Richard, Life for Life's Sake (1941), Cassell, 1968

Bagnold, Enid, A Diary without Dates (1918), Virago Press,
    1978

Blunden, Edmund, Undertones of War, Cobden Trust/
    Sanderson Books, 1928

Chapman, Guy, Vain Glory, Cassell, 1968

Coppard, George, With a Machine Gun to Cambrai, HMSO,
    1969

Delaney, Paul, D. H. Lawrence's Nightmare, Harvester Press,
    1979

Edmonds, Charles, A Subaltern's War, Peter Davies Ltd,
    1929

Graves, Robert, Goodbye to All That (1929), Penguin Books,
    1960

Hurd, Michael, The Ordeal of Ivor Gurney, Oxford University
    Press, 1978

Lewis, Cecil, Sagittarius Rising (1936), Penguin Books, 1977

Lewis, Wyndham, Blasting and Bombardiering, (1937), John
    Calder, 1982

Middlebrook, Michael (ed.), The Diaries of Pte. Horace
    Brookshaw, Scolar Press, 1979

Mizener, A., The Saddest Story, The Bodley Head, 1971

Mottram, R. H.; Easton, John; Partridge, Eric, Three
    Personal Records of the War, Scholartis, 1929

Nevinson, Charles, Paint and Prejudice, Methuen & Co.,
    1937

Sassoon, Siegfried, *The Complete Memoirs of George Sherston,* Faber and Faber, 1937
The Old Century, Faber and Faber, 1938
The Weald of Youth, Faber and Faber, 1942
Siegfried's Journey, Faber and Faber, 1945
Waugh, Evelyn, *A Little Learning,* Chapman and Hall, 1964

Criticism

Cooperman, Stanley, *World War I and the American Novel,* Oxford University Press, 1961
Falls, Cyril, *War Books – a Critical Guide,* Peter Davies Ltd, 1930
Fussell, Paul, *The Great War and Modern Memory* (1975), Oxford University Press, 1979
Greicus, M. S., *Prose Writers of World War I,* Writers and Their Work, 231, Longman, 1973
Johnston, John, *English Poetry of the First World War,* Princeton University Press, 1964
Klein, Holger (ed.), *The First World War in Fiction,* Macmillan, 1978
Lucas, John, *Arnold Bennett,* Methuen & Co., 1974
Modern English Poetry, Batsford, 1986
Williams, Raymond, *The English Novel from Dickens to Lawrence,* Chatto and Windus, 1970

General

Aldington, Richard, *Artifex,* Chatto and Windus, 1935
Angell, Norman, *The Great Illusion,* William Heinemann, 1908
Beaver, Patrick (ed.), *The Wipers Times,* Peter Davies Ltd, 1973
Boulton, David, *Objection Overruled,* MacGibbon and Kee, 1967
Bunyan, John, *Pilgrim's Progress,* J. M. Dent & Sons, 1964

[153]

Ceadel, Martin, *Pacifism in Britain, 1914–45,* Oxford
  University Press, 1980
Cruttwell, C. R. M. F., *A History of the Great War,* Oxford
  University Press, 1970
Gibbs, Philip, *Ten Years After,* Hutchinson & Co., 1924
Girouard, Mark, *The Return to Camelot,* Yale University
  Press, 1981
Haste, Cate, *Keep the Home Fires Burning,* Allen Lane, 1977
Jones, David, *In Parenthesis* (1937), Faber and Faber, 1963
Kunitz, S. and Haycroft, H. (eds.), *Twentieth Century Writers,*
  Wilson, 1942
Laffin, John (ed.), *Letters from the Front,* J. M. Dent & Sons,
  1973
Lamb, David, *Mutinies: 1917–1920,* Solidarity (London), n.d.
Lee, Dwight (ed.), *The Outbreak of the First World War,* D. C.
  Heath and Co., 1966
Leed, Eric, *No Man's Land,* Cambridge University Press, 1979
Liddell Hart, Basil, *History of the First World War* (1934),
  Book Club Associates, 1973
Peterson, H. C., *Propaganda for War,* D. Norman, 1939
Read, J. H., *Atrocity Propaganda,* Yale University Press, 1941
Steiner, Zara, *Britain and the Origins of the First World War,*
  Macmillan, 1977
Tawney, R. H., *The Attack and Other Papers,* George Allen
  and Unwin, 1953
Terraine, John, *To Win a War,* Sidgwick and Jackson, 1978
Thompson, Paul, *The Edwardians* (1975), Paladin Books,
  1977
Tuchman, Barbara, *The Proud Tower* (1966), Macmillan,
                 1980
                 August 1918 (1962), Macmillan, 1980
Wiener, M. J., *English Culture and the Decline of the
  Industrial Spirit 1850–1980* (1981), Penguin Books, 1985
Wilkinson, Alan, *Dissent or Conform? War, Peace and the
  English Churches 1900–1945,* SCM Press, 1985
Wohl, Robert, *The Generation of 1914,* Weidenfeld and
  Nicolson, 1980
Wolff, Leon, *In Flanders Fields* (1959), Penguin Books, 1979

Index